'I love reading Simenon. He makes me think of Chekhov'
— William Faulkner

'A truly wonderful writer . . . marvellously readable – lucid,
simple, absolutely in tune with the world he creates'
— Muriel Spark

'Few writers have ever conveyed with such a sure touch, the
bleakness of human life'   – A. N. Wilson

'One of the greatest writers of the twentieth century.
Simenon was unequalled at making us look inside, though
the ability was masked by his brilliance at absorbing us
obsessively in his stories'   – *Guardian*

'A novelist who entered his fictional world as if he were part
of it'   – Peter Ackroyd

'The greatest of all, the most genuine novelist we have had
in literature'   – André Gide

'Superb. The most addictive of writers. A unique teller of
tales'   – *Observer*

'The mysteries of the human personality are revealed in all
their disconcerting complexity'   – Anita Brookner

'A writer who, more than any other crime novelist, combined
a high literary reputation with popular appeal'   – P. D. James

'A supreme writer. Unforgettable vividness'   – *Independent*

'Compelling, remorseless, brilliant'   – John Gray

'Extraordinary masterpieces of the twentieth century'
— John Banville

GEORGES SIMENON

Maigret and the Killer

Translated by SHAUN WHITESIDE

PENGUIN BOOKS

PENGUIN CLASSICS

UK | USA | Canada | Ireland | Australia
India | New Zealand | South Africa

Penguin Books is part of the Penguin Random House group of companies
whose addresses can be found at global.penguinrandomhouse.com.

First published in French as *Maigret et le tueur* by Presses de la Cité 1969
This translation first published 2019

003

Set in 12.5/15 pt Dante MT Std
Typeset by Jouve (UK), Milton Keynes
Printed and bound in Great Britain by Clays Ltd, Elcograf S.p.A.

ISBN: 978–0–241–30426–6

Maigret and the Killer

1.

For the first time since they had been going for dinner with the Pardons once a month, Maigret had a memory of the evening at Boulevard Voltaire that was almost painful. It had started in Boulevard Richard-Lenoir. His wife had phoned for a taxi, because for three days it had, according to the radio, been raining harder than at any time in the past thirty-five years. The rain was coming down in sheets, frozen, lashing people's hands and faces, making their wet clothes stick to their bodies.

On the stairs, in lifts and offices, feet left dark prints, and everyone was in a terrible mood.

They had gone downstairs and spent almost half an hour on the doorstep, increasingly numb with cold, waiting for the taxi to arrive. Then, on top of everything, they had had to haggle for the driver to agree to take them such a short distance.

'I'm sorry. We're late.'

'Everybody's late these days. Would you mind if we sat down at the table straight away.'

The apartment was warm and intimate, and they felt all the better for the sound of the storm rattling the shutters. Madame Pardon had made her unparalleled boeuf bourguignon, and the dish, filling yet refined, had been the focus of their conversation.

Then they had talked about provincial cookery, about *cassoulet* and *potée Lorraine*, about *tripes à la mode de Caën* and *bouillabaisse*.

'Basically most of these recipes were born of necessity. If they had had refrigerators in the Middle Ages . . .'

What else had they talked about? The two women, as usual, had ended up going to sit in a corner of the sitting room, where they chatted in low voices. Pardon had taken Maigret into his surgery to show him a rare edition given to him by one of his patients. They had sat down in their usual places, and Madame Pardon had come to bring them coffee and calvados.

Pardon was tired. For quite a long time his features had been drawn, and sometimes a kind of resignation appeared in his eyes. He still worked fifteen hours a day, without a word of complaint or recrimination, in his surgery in the morning, and spent part of the afternoon lugging his heavy medical bag from street to street, then back home, where the waiting room was always full.

'If I had a son and he'd told me he intended to become a doctor, I think I would try to dissuade him.'

Maigret nearly looked away out of modesty. Coming from Pardon, these words were most unexpected, because he was passionate about his profession, and it was impossible to imagine him practising another one.

This time, though, he was discouraged and pessimistic, and most importantly he was going so far as to express that pessimism.

'They're turning us into civil servants, and transforming medicine into a big machine for producing basic treatment.'

4

Maigret studied him, lighting his pipe.

'Not only civil servants,' the doctor continued, 'but bad civil servants, because we can no longer devote the necessary time to each patient. Sometimes I'm ashamed as I guide them to the door, nearly pushing them. I see their worried, even imploring faces. I feel that they expected something from me, questions, words, minutes, in short, during which I would attend to their case.'

He raised his glass.

'Your good health.'

He tried to smile, a mechanical smile that didn't suit him.

'Do you know how many patients I've seen today? Eighty-two. And that's not exceptional. After which they make us fill in various forms that take up our evenings. I'm sorry for boring you with that. You must have worries of your own at Quai des Orfèvres.'

What had they talked about after that? The sort of mundane matters that you don't remember the next day. Pardon was sitting at his desk, smoking his cigarette, Maigret in the stiff armchair reserved for the patients. The air was filled with a particular smell with which he was very familiar, because he encountered it every time he visited. A smell that in a way reminded him of the offices at the station. A smell of poverty.

Pardon's patients were local, almost all of them from a very modest background.

The door opened. Eugénie, the maid, who had worked at Boulevard Voltaire for so long that she was more or less part of the family, announced:

'It's the Italian, sir.'

'Which Italian? Pagliati?'

'Yes, sir. He's in a terrible state. Apparently it's very urgent.'

It was 10.30. Pardon got to his feet and opened the door of the sad waiting room, in which magazines were scattered over a pedestal table.

'What's wrong, Gino?'

'It's not me, doctor. Nor my wife. There's a wounded man on the pavement who seems to be dying.'

'Where?'

'Rue Popincourt, less than a hundred metres from here.'

'Was it you who found him?'

Pardon was already in the doorway, putting on his black overcoat, looking for his doctor's bag, and Maigret, quite naturally, put on his coat as well. The doctor opened the door to the sitting room.

'We'll be back right away. An injured man on Rue Popincourt.'

'Take your umbrella.'

He didn't take it. It would have seemed ridiculous, holding an umbrella as he leaned over a man dying in the middle of the pavement in the pelting rain.

Gino was a Neapolitan. He kept a grocer's shop on the corner of Rue du Chemin-Vert and Rue Popincourt. More precisely, it was his wife, Lucia, who kept the shop while he made fresh pasta in the back room, ravioli and tortellini. The couple were popular in the area. Pardon had treated Gino for high blood pressure in the past.

The pasta-maker was a short man with a heavy, thick body and a flushed face.

'We were coming back from my brother-in-law's in Rue de Charonne. My sister-in-law is going to have a baby, and we're expecting to drive her to the maternity hospital at any moment. We were walking in the rain when I saw . . .'

Half of his words were lost in the storm. The gutters were real torrents that you had to jump over, and the few cars sent dirty water spraying several metres.

The spectacle that awaited him in Rue Popincourt was unexpected. There were no pedestrians from one end of the street to the other, and only a few windows, apart from that of a small café, were still lit.

About fifty metres from that café, a stout woman stood motionlessly beneath an umbrella shaken by the wind, and the light from a streetlamp revealed the shape of a body lying at her feet.

It brought back old memories for Maigret. Even before he had been at the head of the Crime Squad, while he had only been an inspector, he had sometimes been first on the scene of a brawl, a settling of scores, a knife attack.

The man was young. He looked barely twenty, he was wearing a suede jacket, and his hair was quite long at the back. He had fallen forwards, and the back of his jacket was stained with blood.

'Have you called the police?'

Pardon, crouching beside the injured man, interrupted:

'Tell them to send an ambulance.'

That meant that the stranger was alive, and Maigret moved towards the light that he could see fifty metres away. Inscribed on the faintly lit display window were the words: 'Chez Jules'. He pushed the glass door, hung with a cream-coloured curtain, and stepped into an atmosphere so calm that it was almost unreal. It was like a genre painting.

It was a bar in the old style, with sawdust on the floor and a strong smell of wine and spirits. Four middle-aged men, three of them fat and red-faced, were playing cards.

'Can I make a phone call?'

They watched with surprise as he walked towards the telephone on the wall, beside the zinc bar and the rows of bottles.

'Hello ... Is that the station of the eleventh arrondissement?'

It was a stone's throw away, at Place Léon-Blum, formerly Place Voltaire.

'Hello. This is Maigret. There's an injured man in Rue Popincourt. Towards Rue du Chemin-Vert. We need an ambulance.'

The four men grew animated, like figures in a painting coming to life. They kept the cards in their hands.

'What is it?' asked someone in shirt-sleeves, who must have been the owner. 'Who's injured?'

'A young man.'

Maigret set some change down on the counter and headed towards the door.

'A tall, thin guy in a suede jacket?'

'Yes.'

'He was here a quarter of an hour ago.'

'On his own?'

'Yes.'

'Did he look nervous?'

The owner, probably Jules, glanced quizzically at the others.

'No. Not especially.'

'Did he stay for long?'

'About twenty minutes.'

When Maigret was outside, he saw two officers on bicycles, capes dripping, standing near the injured man. Pardon had got back to his feet.

'There's nothing I can do. He's been stabbed several times. They missed his heart. And none of his arteries has been cut either, at first glance, or there would have been more blood.'

'Will he regain consciousness?'

'I don't know. I don't dare to move him. Until we get him to a hospital they won't be able to . . .'

The two vehicles, the police car and the ambulance, arrived almost simultaneously. The card-players, rather than getting wet, stood in the doorway of the little café and watched from a distance. Only the owner came over, with a sack over his head and shoulders. He recognized the man's jacket straight away.

'That's him.'

'He didn't say anything to you?'

'No. Except to order a cognac.'

Pardon gave instructions to the orderlies who were bringing their stretcher.

'What's that?' asked one of the police officers, pointing to a black object that looked like a camera.

The injured man wore it across his body. It wasn't a

camera, but a tape recorder. It was drenched with rain, and when the man was being slipped on to the stretcher, Maigret took advantage of the fact to release the strap.

'To Saint-Antoine.'

Pardon got into the ambulance with one of the orderlies while the other one took the wheel.

'Who are you?' he asked Maigret.

'Police.'

'If you want to get in beside me . . .'

The area was deserted, and, less than five minutes later, the ambulance, followed by one of the police vans, reached Saint-Antoine Hospital.

Here too, Maigret found old memories: the globe-shaped light above reception, the long, badly lit corridors where two or three people were waiting on benches in silent resignation, giving a start every time a door opened and closed, or when a man or a woman in white moved from one place to another.

'Do you have his name or address?' asked a matron enclosed in her glass cage with a counter in front of it.

'Not yet.'

A doctor, alerted by a bell, approached from the end of the corridor, reluctantly stubbing out his cigarette. Pardon introduced himself.

'Have you done anything?'

The injured man, lying on a trolley, was being pushed into a lift, and Pardon, who followed it, made a vague gesture to Maigret from a distance as if to say: 'I'll be back in a minute.'

'Do you know anything, inspector?'

'No more than you do. I was having dinner with a friend in the area, when someone came and told my friend, who is a doctor, that there was an injured man lying on the pavement in Rue Popincourt.'

The officer jotted this down in his notebook. Less than ten minutes passed in a disagreeable silence, and Pardon reappeared at the end of the corridor. It was a bad sign. The doctor's face was anxious.

'Dead?'

'Even before they had time to undress him ... Haemorrhage in the pleural cavity. I feared as much when I heard his breathing.'

'Was he stabbed?'

'Yes. Several times. Quite a thin blade. In a few minutes we'll bring you the contents of his pockets. Then, I suppose they'll send them to the Forensic Institute.'

This version of Paris was familiar to Maigret. He had experienced it over the years and yet he had never completely got used to it. What was he doing here? A knife blow, several knife blows, that didn't concern him. That happened every night, and in the morning it would be summed up in three or four lines in the daily reports.

By chance he had had a ringside view, and he also felt somewhat involved. The Italian pasta-maker hadn't had time to tell him what he had seen. He must have gone home with his wife. They slept on the first floor, above the shop.

A nurse came towards the little group, holding a basket.

'Who's in charge of the investigation?'

The plainclothes officers looked at Maigret, and she spoke to him:

'This is what I found in his pockets. You'll have to sign for it.'

There was a small wallet of the kind that can be slipped into the back pocket, a ball-point pen, a pipe, a tobacco pouch containing some very pale Dutch tobacco, a handkerchief, some change and two cassette tapes.

The wallet contained an identity card and a driver's licence in the name of Antoine Batille, twenty-one, with an address at Quai d'Anjou in Paris. It was on the Ile Saint-Louis, not far from Pont Marie. There was also a student card.

'Now then, Pardon, will you ask my wife to go home without me and go to bed?'

'Are you going over there?'

'I'll have to. He probably lives with his parents and I have to inform them.'

He turned towards the policemen.

'You could question Pagliati, the Italian grocer in Rue Popincourt, and the four men who were playing cards at Chez Jules, if they're still at the café.'

As always, he regretted not being able to do everything by himself. He would have liked to go back to Rue Popincourt and go into the little café, were there was something like a fog around the globe light, and where the card-players had probably resumed their game.

He would have liked to question the Italian, his wife, perhaps a little old woman that he had only glimpsed at a lit window on a first floor. Had she already been there when the tragedy had occurred?

But first of all the parents had to be informed. He called

the duty inspector at the eleventh arrondissement and told him what had happened.

'Did he suffer a lot?' he asked Pardon.

'I don't think so. He lost consciousness straight away. There was nothing I could do, there on the pavement.'

The wallet was of excellent-quality crocodile skin, the ball-point pen was silver, the handkerchief hand-embroidered with an A.

'Would you be so kind as to call me a taxi?' he asked the nurse.

She did so, from her cage, without a hint of courtesy. Admittedly it couldn't have been pleasant spending whole nights in so gloomy a place, waiting for local tragedies to wind up at the hospital.

Miraculously, the taxi arrived less than three minutes later.

'I'll drop you off home, Pardon.'

'I don't want to hold you up.'

'You know, with this news I have to deliver . . .'

He knew the Ile Saint-Louis from when they had lived on Place des Vosges, and at that time they had often walked arm in arm around the island in the evening.

He rang at a green door. Cars were lined up along the pavements, most of them luxury models. A narrow door opened up in the larger one.

'Monsieur Batille, please?' he asked, stopping by a kind of skylight.

A sleepy woman's voice replied simply:

'Second on the left.'

He took the lift, and some of the rain drenching his

overcoat and trousers formed a puddle at his feet. The building, like most of the ones on the island, had been restored. The walls were white stone, the lighting came from torches in carved bronze. On the marble landing, the doormat bore a big red letter *B*.

He pressed the button and heard an electric bell ringing very far away, but a very long time passed before the door opened silently.

A young parlour-maid in a fashionable uniform looked at him curiously.

'I'd like to talk to Monsieur Batille.'

'The father or the son?'

'The father.'

'Monsieur and madame haven't come home, and I don't know when they'll be back.'

He showed her his badge. She asked him:

'What is it?'

'Detective Chief Inspector Maigret, of the Police Judiciaire.'

'And you've come to see monsieur at this time of night? Does he know what it's about?'

'No.'

'Is it that urgent?'

'It's important.'

'It's almost midnight. Monsieur and madame have gone to the theatre.'

'In that case, it's possible that they'll be back soon.'

'Unless, as they often do, they go for supper with friends afterwards.'

'Didn't the younger Monsieur Batille go with them?'

'He never goes with them.'

She sounded embarrassed. She didn't know what to do with him, and he must have looked pitiful, dripping with water. He saw a vast hall, its parquet floor covered with a rug, light blue tending slightly towards green.

'If it's really urgent.'

She resigned herself to letting him in.

'Give me your hat and your overcoat.'

She glanced anxiously at his shoes. She still couldn't ask him to take them off.

'This way.'

She hung the coat up in a cupboard, and hesitated to bring Maigret into the big drawing room that opened up on the left.

'Would you mind waiting here?'

He understood very clearly. The apartment was luxurious in a way that was almost excessively refined, and rather feminine. The armchairs in the drawing room were white, and the paintings on the wall were from Picasso's blue period, and by Renoir and Marie Laurencin.

The maid, young and pretty, was clearly wondering whether she was supposed to leave him on his own or keep an eye on him, as if she didn't place very much trust in the badge that he had shown her.

'Is Monsieur Batille a businessman?'

'Don't you know him?'

'No.'

'So you don't know that he's the owner of Mylène Perfumes and Beauty Products?'

He knew so little about beauty products! And Madame

Maigret, who only used a small amount of powder, couldn't have kept him up to date.

'How old is he?'

'Forty-four. Forty-five. He looks very young and . . .'

She blushed. She must have been more or less in love with her boss.

'What about his wife?'

'That's her portrait that you'll see if you bend down a little, above the mantelpiece.'

In a blue evening gown. Blue and pale pink seemed to be the colours of the house, as in the paintings of Marie Laurencin.

'I think I hear the lift.'

And in spite of herself she gave a faint sigh of relief.

She talked to them in an undertone, near the door that she had rushed to open. They were a young couple, elegant, apparently carefree, coming home after an evening at the theatre. They each looked in turn, from a distance, at this intruder with the wet shoes and trousers, who had risen clumsily from his chair and was trying to keep his composure.

The man removed his grey coat, beneath which he wore a dinner-jacket, and his wife, beneath her leopard-skin coat, was wearing a cocktail dress of a fine silver mesh. They had about ten metres to walk, maybe less. Batille came over first, taking quick and nervous steps. His wife followed him.

'I'm told you are Detective Chief Inspector Maigret?' he murmured with a frown.

'That's correct.'

'If I am not mistaken, you are the head of the Crime Squad?'

There was a brief and quite unpleasant silence during which Madame Batille tried to guess what was happening; already she had shed the relaxed mood with which she had passed through the door a few moments before.

'Strange time of night to . . . Might this have anything to do with my son?'

'Were you expecting bad news?'

'Not at all. Let's not stay here. Let's go into my office.'

It was the last room, which opened up on to the drawing room. Batille's real office must have been elsewhere, in the Mylène building, which Maigret had often noticed in Avenue Matignon.

The wood of the bookshelves was very light, lemon or sycamore, and the walls were covered with books. The leather armchairs were a very light beige, like the desk accessories. On the desk stood a photograph in a silver frame, showing Madame Batille, with the faces of two children, a boy and girl.

'Have a seat. Have you been waiting for me for a long time?'

'Only ten minutes or so.'

'Can I offer you a drink?'

'No thank you.'

It seemed as if now the man was putting off the moment of hearing what Maigret had to say to him.

'You aren't worried about your son?'

He seemed to think about it for a second.

'No . . . He's a calm and reserved boy, perhaps too calm and reserved.'

'What do you think about the company he keeps?'

'He hardly sees anybody. He's quite the opposite of his sister, who is only eighteen and makes friends easily. He has no friends, no colleagues . . . Has something happened to him?'

'Yes.'

'An accident?'

'If you could put it that way. He was attacked this evening, on the dark pavement of Rue Popincourt.'

'Is he injured?'

'Yes.'

'Seriously?'

'He's dead.'

He would have preferred not to see them, not to witness their abrupt collapse. The chic couple, full of ease and confidence, disappeared. Their clothes no longer came from the grand stylist, the smart tailor. The apartment itself lost its elegance and charm.

Now there was only a man and a woman still struggling to believe in the reality that they were being told about.

'Are you sure that it's my—'

'Antoine Batille, isn't that right?'

Maigret held out the wallet, still drenched with water.

'That's his, yes.'

He automatically lit a cigarette. His hands were trembling. His lips too.

'How did it happen?'

'He came out of a little local bar. He walked about fifty

metres through the squalling rain and someone stabbed him several times from behind.'

The woman grimaced as if she was the one who had been stabbed, and her husband put his arm around her shoulders. He tried to speak but wasn't immediately able to do so. And to say what, in any case? What was running through his head, even if it wasn't his current concern:

'Have they arrested the . . .'

'No.'

'Did he die straight away?'

'Upon arrival at the Saint-Antoine Hospital.'

'Can we go and see him?'

'I would advise you not to go there tonight, but tomorrow morning.'

'Did he suffer?'

'The doctor says not.'

'You should go to bed, Martine. At least lie down in your bedroom.'

He led her away gently but firmly.

'I'll be with you in a moment, inspector.'

Batille was away for almost a quarter of an hour, and when he came back he was very pale, his features drawn, his face expressionless.

'Please, have a seat.'

He was small, thin and nervous. It was as if Maigret's big, heavy bulk made him uneasy.

'You still don't want anything to drink?'

He opened a small bar and took out a bottle and two glasses.

'I won't pretend I don't need it.'

He served himself a whisky and poured some into the second glass.

'A lot of soda?'

And, straight away:

'I don't understand. I can't understand. Antoine was a boy who hid nothing from me, and besides, there was nothing to hide in his life. He was . . . I find it hard to talk about him in the past tense, and yet I'll have to get used to it . . . He was a student. He was studying literature at the Sorbonne. He wasn't part of any group. He didn't have the slightest interest in politics.'

He stared at the tan carpet, arms dangling, and said to himself:

'They've killed my boy. Why? But why?'

'That's what I'm here to find out.'

He looked at Maigret as if for the first time.

'Why did you take the trouble to come here in person? For the police, it's just a run-of-the-mill event, isn't it?'

'Just by chance I was almost at the scene.'

'Did you see anything?'

'No.'

'Did anyone see anything?'

'An Italian grocer, who was going home with his wife. I have brought you the objects I found in your son's pockets, but I forgot his tape recorder.'

The boy's father didn't seem to understand straight away, then he murmured:

'Ah! Yes.'

He nearly smiled.

'That was his passion. You will probably laugh. His sister and I joked with him about it. Other people are wild about photography and go hunting for photogenic faces even under bridges.

'Antoine collected human voices. Often he spent whole evenings doing it. He went into cafés, stations, all kinds of public places and switched on his tape recorder.

'He wore it around his neck, and lots of people thought it was a camera. He had a miniature microphone hidden in his hand.'

At last Maigret had something to cling to.

'Did he ever have any trouble?'

'Only once. He was in a bar near the Quartier des Ternes. Two men were leaning on the counter. Antoine, leaning on his elbows beside them, was discreetly recording.

' "Come on, kid," one of the two men said suddenly.

'He took his tape recorder off him and removed the cassette.

' "I don't know what you're playing at, but if I ever see you round here again, try not to have that thing with you." '

Gérard Batille took a sip and went on:

'Do you think that . . .'

'Anything is possible. We can't rule anything out. Did he often go out voice-hunting?'

'Two or three evenings a week.'

'Always alone?'

'I told you, he had no friends. He called those recordings "human documents".'

'Are there many of them?'

'Maybe a hundred, maybe more. From time to time he would listen to them and erase the ones that didn't work. At what time do you think, tomorrow . . . ?'

'I'll let the hospital know. After eight, at any rate.'

'Could I have the body brought back here?'

'Not straight away.'

The boy's father understood, and his face turned even paler, as if he was imagining the post-mortem.

'Excuse me, inspector, but I . . .'

He couldn't keep going. He needed to be alone, or perhaps go and join his wife, perhaps weep or shout meaningless words into the silence.

He said, as if to himself:

'I don't know what time Minou will be coming back.'

'Who's—?'

'His sister. She's only eighteen but she lives as she pleases. I imagine you have a coat.'

The maid appeared just as they reached the cupboard and helped Maigret to put on his wet overcoat and held out his hat.

He found himself on the stairs, then passed through the little door and stayed there for a while, watching the rain come down. The wind seemed to have subsided a little, the torrents of rain were less furious. He hadn't dared to ask permission to ring for a taxi.

Shoulders hunched, he crossed Pont Marie, took narrow Rue Saint-Paul and eventually found a taxi parked outside Saint-Paul Métro station.

'Boulevard Richard-Lenoir.'

'Got it, chief.'

Someone who knew him and didn't protest that it was too short a journey. Raising his head, once he had got out of the car, he noticed light in the windows of his apartment. As he was climbing the last flight of stairs, the door opened.

'I hope you haven't caught a cold.'

'I don't think so.'

'I've got some boiling water to make you a hot rum. Sit down. Let me take your shoes off.'

His socks needed wringing out. She went and fetched him a pair of slippers.

'Pardon told his wife and me. How did the parents react? Why did you have to . . . ?'

'I don't know.'

He had attended to the matter automatically, because it had happened almost right in front of him, because it reminded him of so many years that he had spent in the streets of Paris at night.

'They didn't grasp it straight away. They'll both be going to pieces now.'

'Are they young?'

'The man must be a bit over forty-five, but I would say less than fifty. His wife looks barely forty and she's very pretty. You know Mylène perfumes?'

'Of course. Everyone—'

'Well, it's them.'

'They're very rich. They have a chateau in the Sologne, a yacht in Cannes and they give glittering parties.'

'How do you know?'

'You forget that I sometimes spend hours waiting for you, and I sometimes read the newspaper gossip columns.'

She poured some rum into a glass, added some sugar, left in the spoon so that the glass didn't shatter and added boiling water.

'A slice of lemon?'

'No.'

The room felt small and cramped. He looked around at the decor like someone coming back from a long journey.

'What are you thinking about?'

'As you said, they're very rich. They live in one of the most sumptuous apartments I've ever seen. They were coming back from the theatre, still in high spirits. They saw me sitting at the end of the hall. The maid told them in a low voice who I was.'

'Take your clothes off.'

In the end, weren't he and his wife better off here? He put on his pyjamas and went to brush his teeth, and a quarter of an hour later, a little light-headed because of the rum, he was in bed next to Madame Maigret.

'Goodnight,' she said, bringing her face close to his.

He kissed her, as he had done for so many years, and murmured:

'Goodnight.'

'As usual?'

That meant:

'Shall I wake you up at seven thirty as usual, with your coffee?'

He muttered an already vague 'yes', because sleep had

suddenly hit him. He didn't dream. At any rate, if he did, he didn't remember it. And all of a sudden it was morning.

As he drank his coffee, sitting up in bed, and his wife opened the curtains, he tried to see through the tulle covering the lower parts of the windows.

'Is it still raining?'

'No. But judging by the way the men are walking with their hands deep in their pockets, it isn't spring yet, whatever the calendar says.'

It was 19 March. A Wednesday. His first task was to telephone the Saint-Antoine Hospital, and he had a great deal of trouble getting through to a member of the administrative staff.

'Yes. I would like him to be put in a special room . . . I know he's dead. That's no reason for his parents to go and see him in the basement. They'll be there in an hour or two. After their visit, the body will be transferred to the Forensic Institute . . . Yes. Don't worry. The family will pay . . . Yes. They will fill in as many forms as you like.'

He sat down opposite his wife and ate two croissants while drinking a fresh cup of coffee and looking mechanically into the street. There were still clouds moving very low in the sky, but they weren't the same unhealthy colour as the previous day. The wind, which was still strong, shook the branches of the trees.

'Do you have any idea . . . ?'

'You know I never have ideas.'

'And if you do you never say so. Didn't you think Pardon looked terrible?'

'Did you notice that too? He isn't just tired, he's getting pessimistic. Yesterday he talked to me about his profession as he has never done before.'

At nine o'clock he was in his office, and called the eleventh arrondissement station.

'Maigret here. Is that you, Louvelle?'

He had recognized his voice.

'I expect you're calling about the tape recorder?'

'Yes. Have you got it?'

'Demarie collected it and brought it here. I was worried that the rain might have ruined it, but I got it working. I wonder why the boy recorded these conversations.'

'Can you send me the recorder this morning?'

'At the same time as the report, which will be typed up in a few minutes.'

Some mail. Some filing. The previous evening, he hadn't told Pardon that he too was weighed down under administrative paperwork.

Then he went to the morning briefing in the commissioner's office. In a few words he gave an account of what had happened the previous day; because of Gérard Batille's celebrity the case risked causing a stir.

In fact, when he got back to his office, he bumped into a group of journalists and photographers.

'Is it true that you almost witnessed a murder?'

'I only got to the scene quite quickly because I was very close by.'

'Is it true that this boy, Antoine Batille, is the son of Batille the perfume-maker?'

How had the press found out? Did the leak come from the station?

'The concierge says—'

'Which concierge?'

'The one in Quai d'Anjou.'

He hadn't even seen her. He hadn't given her his name, or his title. The maid must have talked.

'It was you who told the parents, wasn't it?'

'Yes.'

'How did they react?'

'Like a man and a woman who are being informed that their son has been killed.'

'Do they suspect anyone?'

'No.'

'Don't you think it might be a political matter?'

'Definitely not.'

'A love affair, then?'

'I don't think so.'

'And nothing was taken, was it?'

'No.'

'So?'

'So, nothing, gentlemen. The investigation is just beginning, and when it has yielded some results, I'll pass them on.'

'Have you seen the daughter?'

'Who?'

'Minou. The Batilles' daughter. Apparently she's famous in certain well-heeled circles.'

'I haven't seen her, no.'

'She keeps strange company.'

'You tell me that, but I'm not investigating her.'

'You never know, do you.'

He forced his way through them, pushed open the door of his office and closed it again. He gave himself enough time to fill a pipe, standing by the window, and then opened the door to the inspectors' office. They weren't all there yet. Some were making phone calls, others typing up their reports.

'Are you busy, Janvier?'

'Another ten lines to type, chief, and I'll be done.'

'Come and see me.'

While he was waiting, he phoned the forensic doctor who had replaced his old friend Dr Paul.

'We'll send it to you towards the end of the morning . . . Yes, it's urgent, less because I'm waiting for the post-mortem than because the parents are impatient . . . Do as little damage to him as possible . . . Yes . . . That's right . . . I see you understand . . . Much of Paris high society will pass to pay their respects. I've already got journalists in the corridor.'

The first thing was to go to Rue Popincourt. The previous day, Gino Pagliati hadn't had time to tell him much, and his wife had barely opened her mouth. Then there were the man called Jules and the three other card-players. Finally, Maigret remembered the silhouette of the old woman he had seen at a window.

'What are we doing, chief?' Janvier asked as he came into the office.

'Is there a free car in the courtyard?'

'I hope so.'

'Drive me to Rue Popincourt. Not far from Rue du Chemin-Vert. I'll tell you where to stop.'

His wife was right, he noticed as he waited for the car in the middle of the courtyard: it was as cold as December.

2.

Maigret realized that Janvier himself was rather surprised about the importance given to this case. Every night, a certain number of stabbings are recorded somewhere in Paris, particularly in busy areas, and normally the papers would only have devoted a few lines to the tragedy in Rue Popincourt under the heading 'other news'.

Stabbings

A young man, Antoine B—, 21, a student, was stabbed several times while walking along Rue Popincourt at about 10.30. The crime appears to have been the work of a prowler, and the approach of a pair of local shopkeepers prevented him from robbing the victim. Antoine B— succumbed to his injuries upon arrival at Saint-Antoine Hospital.

Except that Antoine B. was called Batille and he lived on the Quai d'Anjou. His father was a well-known figure in Paris society, and almost everyone knew Mylène perfumes.

The little black police car crossed Place de la République, and Maigret found himself in his own district, a network of narrow, busy streets bounded by Boulevard Voltaire on one side and Boulevard Richard-Lenoir on the other.

He and Madame Maigret crossed those little streets every time they came to the Pardons for dinner, and Madame Maigret often did her shopping in Rue du Chemin-Vert.

It was at Gino's, as the shop was commonly known, that she bought not only pasta, but mortadella, prosciutto from Milan and olive oil in big gold cans. The shops were narrow, deep and badly lit. Today, because of the overcast sky, almost all the lamps were lit, creating a fake daylight that made people's faces look like waxworks.

A lot of old women. A lot of middle-aged men, too, on their own, carrying a basket of provisions. Resigned faces. Some of them stopped occasionally and brought a hand to their heart as they waited for the end of a spasm.

Women of every nationality, with a young child in their arms and a boy or a little girl clinging to their dress.

'Stop here and come with me.'

He started with the Pagliatis. There were three women customers in the shop, and Lucia was busy.

'My husband's at the back. Just push the little door.'

Gino was busy making ravioli on a long marble slab covered with flour.

'My goodness! Inspector, I thought you would come.'

He had a loud voice, and naturally radiant features.

'Is it true that the poor boy is dead?'

The news wasn't yet in the papers.

'Who told you that?'

'A journalist who was here ten minutes ago. He took my photograph, and I'll be seeing my portrait in the paper.'

'I would like you to repeat to me what you said last night, in as much detail as possible. You were coming back from seeing your brother and sister-in-law . . .'

'. . . Who is expecting a baby, yes. Rue de Charonne. We had only brought one umbrella for both of us because, when we walk in the street, Lucia always takes my arm.

'You remember the rain that was coming down, a storm. Several times I thought the umbrella was going to turn inside out, and I was holding it in front of us like a shield.

'Which explains why I didn't see him sooner.'

'Who?'

'The killer. He must have been walking in front of us, a certain distance away, but I was only concerned with protecting us from the rain and not wading in the puddles. He might also have been standing in a doorway.'

'When did you notice him?'

'He was already past Chez Jules, where the light was still on.'

'Could you see how he was dressed?'

'I talked to my wife about that last night. We both think he was wearing a light-coloured mackintosh with a belt. He had a quick, agile way of walking.'

'Did he seem to be following the young man in the jacket?'

'He was moving faster than him, as if to catch up with him or overtake him.'

'How far were you from the two men?'

'Perhaps a hundred metres. I could go and show you.'

'Did the one who was walking ahead turn round?'

'No. The other man caught up with him. I saw his arm going up and coming down. I couldn't make out the knife. He struck three or four times, and the young man in the jacket fell forwards on to the pavement. The murderer took a few steps towards Rue du Chemin-Vert, then came back. He must have seen us, because we were only about sixty metres away. He even bent down and stabbed him two or three more times.'

'You didn't chase him?'

'You know, I'm quite stout and I suffer from emphysema. It isn't easy for me to run.'

He was blushing, embarrassed.

'We quickened our step, and this time he vanished around the corner of the street.'

'Did you hear the sound of a car starting?'

'I don't think so . . . I didn't notice . . .'

Mechanically, and without Maigret having to tell him to, Janvier was jotting down the conversation in shorthand.

'And when you reached the wounded man . . . ?'

'You saw him just as I left him. His jacket was torn in several places, and we could see blood flowing. I immediately thought about calling a doctor and rushed to Dr Pardon's house, asking Lucia to stay there.'

'Why?'

'I don't know. I thought we couldn't leave him all alone.'

'Did your wife say anything when you came back?'

'As if on purpose, no one passed by.'

'The injured man didn't speak?'

'No. He was breathing badly, with a gurgle in his

chest. Lucia will be able to tell you. She's at her busiest right now.'

'No other detail occurs to you?'

'No. I've told you everything I know.'

'Thank you, Gino.'

'How is Madame Maigret?'

'Very well, thank you.'

An alleyway to the side led to a courtyard, where, behind glass, a welder was working in his studio. The district was full of such courtyards and cul-de-sacs, all of them with small craftsmen's workshops.

They crossed the street and, a little further on, Maigret pushed open the door of Chez Jules. By day, the little café was almost as dark as it was in the evening, and the milky globe lamp was lit. A bulky man whose shirt poked out between his trousers and his waistcoat was leaning on the bar. He had a flushed complexion, a thick neck and a goitrous-looking double chin.

'What can I get you, Monsieur Maigret? A glass of Sancerre? It comes from my cousin, who . . .'

'Two,' Maigret said, leaning in turn on the counter.

'Today, you're not the first.'

'A journalist, I know.'

'He took my photograph, as I am now, holding a bottle. You know Lebon. He worked in the highways department for thirty years. Then he had an accident, and now he's drawing his pension, plus a little allowance because of his eye. He was here last night.'

'There were four of you playing cards, isn't that right?'

'A game of *manille*. Always the same players every evening except Sunday. I'm closed on Sundays.'

'Are you married?'

'My wife's upstairs, she's ill.'

'At what time did the young man come in?'

'It must have been ten o'clock.'

Maigret glanced at the advertising clock on the wall.

'Ignore that. It's twenty minutes fast . . . First of all he opened the door a few centimetres, as if to see what kind of place it was. It was a lively game. The butcher was winning, and when he's winning he gets insulting, as if he's the only one who knows how to play.'

'So he came in. And then?'

'I asked him, from my seat, what he wanted to drink, and, after hesitating, he murmured:

' "Do you have any cognac?"

'I waited until I'd played the four cards that I was still holding and went behind the bar. As I served him, I noticed a kind of triangular black box that he was wearing over his stomach, hanging around his neck, and I said to myself that it must have been a camera. Sometimes tourists get lost around here, but not very often.

'I went back to my seat at the table. Baboeuf dealt the cards. The young man didn't seem to be in a hurry. He wasn't interested in the game either.'

'Did he seem anxious?'

'No.'

'Did he face the door as if he was waiting for somebody?'

'Not that I noticed.'

'Or as if he was afraid of seeing somebody bursting in?'

'No. He stood where he was with his elbow on the bar, and from time to time he sipped from his glass.'

'What impression did he make on you?'

'Well, he was drenched. With his jacket and his long hair he looks like some young people you see these days.

'We went on playing as if he wasn't there, and Baboeuf was becoming more and more excited because he kept getting a good hand.

' "Maybe you should go home and see what your wife's up to," Lebon joked.

' "Perhaps you should think about your own wife, who's a bit too pretty for you, and who . . ."

'For a moment I thought a fight was going to break out. It calmed down, as it always does. Baboeuf played his hand.

' "What do you think of that?"

'Then Lebon, who was on the banquette beside me, elbowed me in the ribs and nodded towards the customer standing at the bar. I looked at him, not understanding. He looked as if he was laughing to himself. Isn't that right, François? I wondered what you were trying to show me. You said to me in a low voice:

' "Just now." '

And the man with the glass eye took up the story.

'I'd noticed a movement of his hand on the device. I have a nephew who got a thing like that for Christmas, and he enjoys recording what his parents say. He looked like butter wouldn't melt in his mouth, standing there with his glass, but he was listening to everything that we were saying, as the tape went round . . .'

'I wonder,' Jules muttered, 'what he expected to do with that.'

'Nothing. Like my nephew. He records for the sake of it, then he doesn't give it another thought. Once he played one of his parents' arguments back to them, and my brother nearly broke the thing.

' "If I catch you doing that again, you little brat . . ."'

'Baboeuf wouldn't be too happy if you played him back his boasts from yesterday.'

'How long did the young man stay?'

'Just under half an hour.'

'He only had one drink?'

'Yes. He even left a bit of cognac in the bottom of his glass.'

'So he went out, and you didn't hear anything more?'

'Nothing. Just the wind, and the water coming out of the drainpipe, on to the pavement.'

'Did anyone come in before him?'

'You see, in the evening I only stay open for the game, because only these few regulars come in. It only gets crowded in the morning, for coffee, croissants or a glass of white wine with Vichy water. At about ten thirty workmen come in for a break, when there's a building site locally. We do most of our trade before lunch and in the early evening.'

'Thank you.'

Here again, Janvier had jotted down the conversation, and the landlord of the bistro had kept darting little glances at him.

'He didn't teach me anything new,' Maigret sighed. 'He only confirmed what I already knew.'

They returned to their seats in the car. Some women looked at them, because people already knew who they were.

'Where to, chief?'

'To the office, first of all.'

His two visits to Rue Popincourt hadn't been pointless. First of all, there had been the account of the assault from the Neapolitan. Antoine Batille's assailant had stabbed him several times. He had started to move away and then, for some mysterious reason, he had retraced his steps, in spite of the couple a little way off on the pavement. Was it to finish off his victim, whom he had stabbed again before running off?

He was wearing a light-coloured raincoat with a belt; that was all they knew about him. As soon as he reached Quai des Orfèvres, in his office, which was pleasantly warm, Maigret called the Pagliatis' shop.

'Could I have a word with your husband? This is Maigret.'

'I'll call him, inspector.'

And Gino was on the line:

'Hello. How can I help you?'

'Tell me. There's one question that I forgot to ask you. Was the murderer wearing a hat?'

'A journalist has just asked me the same thing. That's the third one since this morning. I had to ask my wife. She's like me. She can't be certain, but she's almost sure that he was wearing a dark hat. You know, it happened so quickly.'

The light-coloured, belted raincoat seemed to indicate quite a young man, while his hat probably added a few years. Not many young people still wore hats these days.

'Tell me, Janvier, I don't suppose you know anything about these contraptions?'

Maigret didn't know anything about them, any more than he knew about photography or cars, which was why his wife did the driving. In the evening, he barely knew how to switch from one television channel to another.

'My son has one just like it.'

'Be careful not to wipe the recording.'

'Don't worry, chief.'

Janvier smiled and pressed some buttons. They heard a hubbub, the sound of forks and plates, a confusion of voices in the distance.

'*And for Madame.*'

'*Do you have boeuf gros sel?*'

'*Of course, Madame.*'

'*With lots of onions and gherkins.*'

'*You know what the doctor told you. No vinegar.*'

'*One minute steak and one boeuf gros sel with lots of onions and gherkins. Would you like salad with that?*'

The recording was far from perfect, and there was a constant background noise that prevented them from making out every word.

A silence. Then a sigh, very distinct.

'*You'll never see sense. Tonight, you'll have to get up and have some bicarbonate of soda.*'

'*Who gets up, you or me? And then, when you go on snoring . . .*'

'*I don't snore.*'

'*You do snore, particularly when you've had a bit too much Beaujolais, as you will do again tonight.*'

'One steak, medium rare. I'll bring the boeuf gros sel straight away.'

'You hardly touch it at home.'

'We aren't at home.'

There were some noises that sounded like gargling. A voice said:

'Waiter! Waiter! Could you finally . . .'

Then silence, as if the tape had been cut. Then a neutral voice said very clearly, because this time it must have been speaking right into the microphone:

'Brasserie Lorraine, Boulevard Beaumarchais.'

Almost definitely the voice of Antoine Batille, stating where the recording had been made. He had probably had his dinner at Boulevard Beaumarchais and discreetly turned on his tape recorder. The waiter would probably remember him. It would be easy to check.

'Go down there later,' Maigret said. 'Turn the tape back on.'

Strange noises, first of all, in the street, because there was the sound of passing cars. For a while Maigret wondered what the young man was trying to record, and it took him a moment to work out that it was the noise of water in the gutters. The sound was hard to identify, but all of a sudden it changed, and again they were in a public place, a café or a bar, with quite a lively atmosphere.

'What did he say to you?'

'That it was OK.'

Some voices, faint but quite distinct.

'Did you go down there, Mimile?'

'Lucien and Gouvion are taking turns . . . In this weather . . .'

'With the car?'

'As usual.'

'Don't you think it's a bit too close?'

'Close to what?'

'To Paris.'

'As long as he doesn't go there until Friday.'

Glasses, cups, more voices. Silence.

'Recorded at the Café des Amis, Place de la Bastille.'

It wasn't far from Boulevard Beaumarchais, and from Rue Popincourt. Batille didn't linger, probably to avoid being noticed, and set off through the rain to find a new place.

'What about your wife? It's easy to talk about other people, but you'd be better off keeping an eye on what's happening at home.'

It must have been the butcher, the card game at Chez Jules.

'Keep your nose out of my business, that's my advice. It's not because you're winning.'

'I'm winning because I don't keep throwing my trumps away like an idiot.'

'Would you two stop it.'

'He started it.'

If the voices had been higher-pitched, it could have been two children arguing.

'Can we get back to the game?'

'I'm not going to play with someone who—'

'He was talking generally, without getting at anyone in particular.'

'Let him say it, if that's how it is.'

Silence.

'*You see. He should keep his trap shut.*'

'*I'm keeping my trap shut because it's all too stupid. Now I'm going to play my cards. Maybe that'll shut you up?*'

The sound was poor. The people talking were too far from the microphone, and Janvier had to play that part of the tape several times. Each time they could make out one or two more words.

Eventually, Batille said:

'*Chez Jules, a little local bistro, Rue Popincourt.*'

'Is that all?'

'That's all.'

The rest of the tape was blank.

Batille must have said his last words on the pavement, a few moments before being assaulted by a stranger.

'And the other two cassettes?'

'They're blank. They're still in their original wrapping. I suppose he was going to use them later.'

'Did you notice anything?'

'The ones from Bastille.'

'Yes. Play that bit again.'

Janvier jotted it down. Then he repeated the few lines that seemed to assume a more precise meaning as they listened.

'It sounds as if there are at least three of them.'

'Yes.'

'And then the two they talked about, Gouvion and Lucien. A bit more than half an hour after his recording, Antoine had been attacked in Rue Popincourt.'

'Except they didn't take his tape recorder off him.'

'Perhaps because the Pagliatis were approaching.'

'I forgot something, in Rue Popincourt. Last night I spotted an old woman at an upstairs window, more or less opposite the scene of the attack.'

'I've got it, chief. Shall I go there right now?'

Maigret, left on his own, went and stood by the window. The Batilles must have gone to Saint-Antoine Hospital, and the forensic doctor would soon take possession of the body.

Maigret still hadn't seen the dead man's sister, whom the family called Minou and who apparently kept strange company.

Convoys of barges glided slowly along the grey Seine, and tugs lowered their funnels as they passed under Pont Saint-Michel.

In the season of bad weather, the terrace was shielded by glazed partitions and heated by two braziers. Around the horseshoe-shaped bar, the room was quite large, the tables tiny, the chairs the kind that cram everybody close together in the evening.

Maigret sat down beside a pillar and, when one of the waiters passed close by, ordered a beer. He absently studied the faces around him. The clientele was quite mixed. At the bar, for example, there were mostly men in blue work overalls, or the local old people who had come for their glass of red wine.

As to the others, the ones who were sitting down, there was a bit of everything: a woman dressed in black, surrounded by her two children and a big suitcase, as if in a station waiting room; a couple holding hands and gazing passionately into each other's eyes; boys with very long hair sniggering and watching after the waitress and teasing her every time she passed by.

Because, as well as the two waiters in the café, there was a waitress with a particularly coarse face. In her black dress, with her white apron, she was thin, her back bent with exhaustion, and she barely managed to raise a smile for the customers.

Some men and women were quite well-dressed, others less so. Some ate a sandwich and drank a coffee or a glass of beer. Others were having an aperitif.

The landlord was standing by the till, dressed in black with a white shirt and black tie, his brown hair carefully stuck to his bald patch, which it covered with an inadequate network of thin, dark lines.

It was his post, evidently, and nothing that happened in his establishment escaped him. He watched the comings and goings of the two waiters and the waitress, while at the same time keeping an eye on the trainee who was putting the bottles and glasses on the trays. Every time he received a token he pressed a button on the till, and a number appeared on the display.

He had plainly been in the restaurant business for a long time, and had probably started out as a waiter himself. Maigret would discover later, when he went down to the toilet, that there was a second, smaller, low-ceilinged room downstairs, where a few customers were drinking.

Here nobody was playing cards or dominoes. It was a place of passing trade, and there couldn't have been many locals. The ones who had been sitting at the table for ages were waiting until it was time for a meeting they were having somewhere nearby.

At last Maigret got to his feet and walked over to the till, without any illusions about the reception he would have.

'Excuse me, sir.'

He discreetly held out his badge in the hollow of his hand.

'Detective Chief Inspector Maigret of the Police Judiciaire.'

The manager's eyes kept their suspicious expression, the same one that he reserved for the waiters and the customers as they went in and out.

'What do you want to know?'

'Were you here yesterday, at about nine thirty?'

'I'd gone to bed. In the evening it's my wife who takes care of the till.'

'Were the same waiters on duty?'

He went on watching after them.

'Yes.'

'I would like to ask them two or three questions about some customers that they might have noticed.'

The man's black eyes stared at him, not very encouragingly.

'We only serve decent people here, and the waiters are very busy at this time of day.'

'I will only need a minute with each of them. Was the waitress here too?'

'No. There aren't so many people in the evening. Jérôme!'

One of the waiters stopped abruptly by the till, holding his tray. The manager turned towards Maigret.

'Go on! Ask your question.'

'Did you notice, last night at around nine thirty, quite a young customer, twenty-one years old, wearing a brown jacket and with a tape recorder around his neck?'

The waiter turned towards the manager, then towards Maigret, and shook his head.

'Do you know a regular who is known to his friends as Mimile?'

'No.'

When it was the turn of the second waiter the results were no more illuminating. They were reluctant to reply, as if they were afraid of the manager, and it was hard to tell if they were being sincere. Maigret, disappointed, returned to his table and ordered a second glass of beer. It was then that he went down to the toilets and, downstairs, found a third waiter, younger than the two up above.

He decided to sit down and order a drink.

'Tell me, do you ever work on the ground floor?'

'Three days out of four. We take turns to be downstairs.'

'Last night?'

'I was upstairs.'

'In the evening too? At about half past nine?'

'Until closing time, at eleven. They closed early, because with this weather there weren't many people in.'

'Did you happen to notice a young man with quite long hair, wearing a suede jacket and with a tape recorder around his neck?'

'Are you sure it was a tape recorder?'

'Did you notice it?'

'Yes. It isn't tourist season yet. I thought it was a camera like the Americans wear. Then a customer asked a question.'

'Which customer?'

'There were three of them at the next table. When the young man left, one of them watched after him with a annoyed, uneasy expression. He called me over:

' "Tell me, Toto."

'Of course, my name isn't Toto, but it's a thing some people say, particularly around here.

' "What did that guy have to drink?"

' "A cognac."

' "You didn't happen to notice if he used his tape machine?"

' "I didn't see him taking photos."

' "Photos my eye! It's a tape recorder, you idiot. Have you ever seen that guy before?"

' "It's the first time."

' "What about me?"

' "I think I've served you three or four times."

' "Fine. Same again." '

The waiter left, because a customer was knocking on his table with a coin to attract his attention. The customer paid. The waiter gave him his change and helped him to put on his overcoat.

Then he came back and paced around Maigret.

'You said there were three of them?'

'Yes. The one who shouted over to me, and who seemed

to be the most important, is a man of about thirty-five, built like a PE teacher, with brown hair and black eyes under thick eyebrows.'

'Is it true that he only came two or three times?'

'I only noticed him those times.'

'What about the others?'

'The redhead with the scar is often in the neighbourhood and comes in to drink a rum at the bar.'

'And the third one?'

'I heard his companions calling him Mimile. I know that one by sight, and I know where he lives. He's a picture-framer with a shop in Faubourg Saint-Antoine, almost on the corner of Rue Trousseau. Rue Trousseau is where I live.'

'Does he come here a lot?'

'I've seen him a few times, I wouldn't say often.'

'With the other two?'

'No. With a little blonde who looks like she's from around here too, a shop-girl or something like that.'

'Thank you. Do you have anything else to tell me?'

'No. If anything comes back to me, or if I see them again . . .'

'In that case call me at the Police Judiciaire. Me or, if I'm not there, one of my colleagues. What's your name?'

'Julien. Julien Blond. My workmates call me Blondinet, because I'm the youngest. When I'm their age, I hope I'll be doing something else for a living.'

Maigret was too close to home to go for lunch at the Brasserie Dauphine. He was almost sorry. He would have liked to take Janvier there and tell him what he had just found out.

'Have you discovered something?' his wife asked him.

'I don't yet know if it's interesting. I have to keep looking.'

At two o'clock he called three of his favourite inspectors into the office, Janvier, Lucas and young Lapointe, who would probably still be called that when he was fifty.

'Turn on the tape recorder, will you, Janvier? You two, listen carefully.'

Lucas and Lapointe pricked up their ears, of course, as soon as the recording made at the Café des Amis began.

'I was there just now. I know the profession and the address of one of the three men who met around a table and talked in an undertone. The one nicknamed Mimile. He's a picture-framer with a shop in Rue du Faubourg Saint-Antoine, two or three houses away from Rue Trousseau.'

Maigret didn't dare to get too excited. It had all gone a bit too quickly for his liking.

'You two, go and organize a stakeout in front of the framer's shop. Get two colleagues to take over from you this evening. If Mimile leaves, someone's got to follow him, ideally two. If he meets somebody, one of you tail him. Similarly, if someone who doesn't look like a customer comes to the shop. In other words, I'd like to know who he might come into contact with.'

'Got it, chief.'

'You, Janvier, look through the files for pictures of men of about thirty-five, well-built, handsome fellows, brown hair, thick brown eyebrows and black eyes. There must be a few, but this is someone who isn't in hiding, who has never been in trouble, or who may have served his sentence.'

Once he was alone in his office he called the Forensic Institute. Dr Desalle came to the phone.

'Maigret here. Have you finished the post-mortem, doctor?'

'Half an hour ago. You know how many times this boy was stabbed? Seven. All in the back. All more or less level with the heart, and yet they missed it.'

'The knife?'

'I was getting to that. The blade isn't wide, but long and pointed. My guess is that it was one of those Swedish knives where the blade comes out when you press a button.

'Only one of those wounds was deadly, the one that perforated the right lung and caused a fatal haemorrhage.'

'Did you notice anything else?'

'The boy was healthy, fit, not very athletic. Egghead type, doesn't take any exercise. All the other organs in excellent condition. His blood contained a certain quantity of alcohol, but he wasn't drunk. He must have drunk two or three glasses of what I think was cognac.'

'Thank you, doctor.'

'You'll get my report tomorrow morning.'

All that was left was routine work. The prosecutor had appointed an examining magistrate, Poiret, with whom Maigret had never worked. Another young man. It struck him that the legal staff had been changing with disconcerting speed for some years. Might it seem that way because of his own age?

He called the magistrate, who told him to come up straight away if he was free. He brought the texts that

Janvier had typed up from the conversations recorded on the tape recorder.

Poiret had had to settle for one of the older offices. Maigret sat down on an uncomfortable chair.

'Pleased to meet you,' said the magistrate, who was tall with fair hair in a crew cut.

'Likewise. Of course, I have come to talk to you about young Batille.'

The magistrate unfolded an afternoon newspaper, with a three-column headline on the front page. Beneath it was the photograph of a young man who hadn't yet grown his hair long, and who looked very much like the son of a 'good family'.

'I gather you've seen the father and mother.'

'I told them the news, yes. They were coming back from the theatre, both in evening dress. If I remember correctly they were practically singing when they came in through the door of their apartment. I have seldom seen two people go to pieces so quickly.'

'Only child?'

'No. There's a sister, an eighteen-year-old girl who sounds like a bit of a handful.'

'Have you seen her?'

'Not yet.'

'What's their apartment like?'

'Very spacious, luxurious and cheerful too. Some old items of furniture, it seemed to me, but not many. The overall effect was modern, but not aggressively so.'

'They must be extremely rich,' the examining magistrate sighed.

'I suppose so.'

'The newspaper story about what happened seems quite fanciful to me.'

'Does it mention the tape recorder?'

'No. Why? Does a tape recorder play an important part?'

'Perhaps. I'm not sure yet. Antoine Batille had a passion for recording conversations in the street, in restaurants and cafés. He saw them as human documents. He led quite a lonely life and often, particularly in the evening, he set off hunting like that, particularly in working-class areas.

'Yesterday he started in a restaurant on Boulevard Beaumarchais, where he recorded scraps of a marital dispute.

'Then he went to a café in Bastille, and this is the text of his recording.'

He held out the piece of paper to the magistrate, who frowned.

'This seems quite compromising, doesn't it?'

'It's obviously about arranging to meet on Thursday evening, somewhere outside a house around Paris. Probably a second home, because the owner won't arrive until Friday and will have to leave on Monday morning.'

'That's what the text suggests, yes.'

'To be sure that the villa will be empty, the gang has it put under surveillance by two of its men in turn. I also know who Mimile is and I have his address.'

'In that case . . .'

The magistrate seemed to be saying that it was all done and dusted, but Maigret was less optimistic.

'If it's the gang I think it is . . .' he began. 'For two years, a number of important villas have had visits from robbers while their owners were in Paris. They almost always took paintings and precious knick-knacks. In Tessancourt they ignored two paintings that were only copies, which indicates—'

'Connoisseurs.'

'A connoisseur, in any case.'

'What's troubling you?'

'That these people haven't killed yet. It's not their style.'

'It can happen, however, as it did last night.'

'Let's imagine that they suddenly suspected the tape recorder was running. It was easy for them to follow Antoine Batille, two of them, for example. Once he was in a deserted street, like Rue Popincourt, all they had to do was jump on him and pull off his tape recorder.'

The magistrate sighed regretfully:

'Clearly.'

'These robbers rarely kill, and when they do it's in desperate cases. They've been working for two years without being caught. We don't even have any idea how they resell the paintings and artworks. That requires at least a brains behind the operation, a man who knows about painting, who has connections, who sets out what needs to be done and perhaps gets involved after assigning a task to each member of the gang.

'This man, who must exist, wouldn't let his accomplices kill.'

'In that case, what do you think?'

'I don't think anything yet. I'm feeling my way. I'm on the trail, of course. Two of my inspectors are keeping an eye on the framing shop that belongs to this man Mimile. Another is searching through the files looking for a thirty-five-year-old individual with thick dark eyebrows.'

'Will you keep me informed?'

'As soon as I know anything.'

Was everything Gino Pagliati said trustworthy? The Neapolitan had said that the murderer had stabbed the victim several times, that he had taken a few steps towards the corner of the street, had come back and struck three more times.

That didn't chime with the hypothesis of a semi-professional either, particularly since in the end he hadn't taken the tape recorder.

Janvier had delivered a report on his visit to the woman he had seen at a first-floor window.

Madame Esparbès, a widow, seventy-two. Lives alone in a three-room apartment with kitchen, where she has been for ten years. Her husband was an officer. She has a pension and lives quite comfortably, but without any luxuries.

Very nervous, she claims that she hardly sleeps these days and, every time she wakes up she is in the habit of going and resting her forehead against the window.

'It's an old woman's obsession, inspector.'

'What did you see last night? Don't worry about going into details, even if they don't seem interesting.'

'I hadn't yet taken my evening bath. At ten o'clock, as usual, I listened to the news on the radio. Then I turned it off and went and stood at the window. I hadn't seen rain like that for a long time, and it brought back old memories. Never mind.

'At about ten thirty, just before, a young man in a jacket came out of the little café opposite and on his chest he was wearing something that looked like quite a large camera. I was quite surprised.

'Almost at the same time I saw another young man.'

'You said: a young man?'

'Yes. Smaller than the first, a little bulkier, but not much. I didn't notice where he came from. In a few quick and probably silent steps he was beside the other man and started striking him several times. I nearly opened the window and called to him to stop, but there would have been no point. The victim was already on the ground. Then the murderer bent over him and lifted his head, grabbing him by the hair to look at him.'

'Are you sure of that?'

'Certain. The streetlamp isn't far away, and I vaguely made out his features.'

'Then?'

'He went away. Then he turned back on himself, as if he had forgotten something. The Pagliatis were walking along the pavement, under their umbrella, about fifty metres away. Even so, he struck the man on the ground three times, then ran off.'

'Did he turn the corner of Rue du Chemin-Vert?'

'Yes. The Pagliatis arrived, then. But you know the rest. I recognized Dr Pardon; I didn't know who was with him.'

'Would you recognize the attacker?'

'Not really. Not his face. Only his frame.'

'And you're sure he was young?'

'I don't think he's over thirty.'

'Long hair?'

'No.'

'Moustache, sideburns?'

'No. I'd have noticed.'

'Was he drenched as if he had been walking in the rain or did he look like he'd just stepped out of a house?'

'They were both drenched. You only needed to be outside for a few minutes to have your clothes soaking.'

'A hat?'

'Yes. A dark hat, probably brown.'

'Thank you.'

'I've told you everything I know, but please don't put my name in the paper. I have nephews in good positions, and they wouldn't want people to know that I live here.'

The phone rang. He recognized Pardon's voice.

'Is that you, Maigret? Am I disturbing you? I didn't expect to find you in your office. I took the liberty of phoning to ask if you have any news.'

'We're following a lead, but there's nothing to say that it's the right one. As for the post-mortem, it confirmed your diagnosis. There was only one fatal blow, the one that pierced the right lung.'

'Do you think it's a financially motivated crime?'

'I don't know. There weren't a lot of prowlers and drunks in the street in this weather. There were no fights.

In the two places where he stopped before going into Chez Jules, young Batille didn't argue with anybody.'

'Thank you. You see, I feel slightly involved in the case. Now, to work. I have eleven patients in my waiting room.'

'Good luck!'

Maigret went and sat in his armchair, chose a pipe from his desk and filled it, his expression vague like the landscape beyond the window, which was slowly filling with fog.

3.

At about 5.30 there was a call from Lucas.

'I thought you'd like me to give you an initial report, chief. I'm in a little bar just opposite the framer's shop. His name's actually Émile Branchu. He moved into Rue du Faubourg Saint-Antoine about two years ago.

'He seems to come from Marseille, but we don't know that for certain. They also say that he was married down there, but that he separated from his wife or divorced.

'He lives alone. An old woman from the area comes and does his cleaning, and he takes most of his meals in a restaurant frequented by locals.

'He has a car, a green 6CV, which he parks in the court-yard closest to his home. He goes out a lot in the evening and comes back in the small hours, often in the company of a pretty girl, never the same one. Not the kind of girls that you find locally or in the nightclubs in the Rue de Lappe. Girls who look like models, in evening dress and furs.

'Is that significant?'

'Of course. Go on.'

Of all his colleagues, Lucas was the oldest, and Maigret was often informal with him. He was also informal with Lapointe, because he had started very young, when he still looked like an overgrown child.

'There were only three customers, two men and a woman. The woman bought a magnifying mirror, because he sells mirrors too. One of the men brought a photographic enlargement for framing and took a long time making his choice.

'The third left with a framed canvas under his arm. I had a clear view of it, because he had come and looked at it closely when it was in the window. It's a landscape with a river, a bit of a daub.'

'Did he make any phone calls?'

'From my post, I can see the phone very clearly, on the counter. He didn't use it. On the other hand, when the newspaper boy passed he came out into the doorway to buy two different papers.'

'Is Lapointe still there?'

'For now he's outside. A door at the back opens up not only on to the courtyard, but on to a network of alleyways like many in the area. Given that he has a car and could use it, it would be a good idea for Lourtie and Neveu to bring a vehicle too when they take over from us.'

'Fine. Thank you.'

Janvier had come back down with about fifteen photographs showing men of about thirty-five with brown hair and thick eyebrows.

'This is all I can find, chief. Do you still need me? One of the kids has a birthday and . . .'

'Wish him a happy birthday from me.'

He went into the inspectors' office, saw Lourtie and told him to take a car to go to Rue du Faubourg Saint-Antoine.

'Where is Neveu?'

'He's in one of the offices. He'll be back soon.'

Maigret had nothing more to do at the office and, with the photographs in his pocket, he went down into the courtyard, passed through the arch, greeted the guard with a wave and headed towards the Boulevard du Palais, where he found a taxi. He wasn't in a bad mood, but he wasn't cheerful either. One might have believed that he was leading this investigation without any conviction, as if something had been skewed from the outset, and it all came back to the scene that had played out under the torrential rain, in the darkness of Rue Popincourt.

Young Batille, coming out of the dimly lit bistro where the four men were playing cards . . . The Pagliatis, under their umbrella, still quite a way down the street . . . Madame Esparbès at her window . . .

And someone, a man of thirty at most, who suddenly appeared on the scene . . . There was no way of telling if he was waiting in a doorway for Antoine Batille to come out, or whether he too had been walking along the pavement . . . He walked quickly for a few metres and then stabbed, once, twice, at least four times . . .

He heard the footsteps of the pasta-maker and his wife, who were less than fifty metres away . . . He walked towards the corner of Rue du Chemin-Vert and, as he turned the corner, he retraced his steps.

Why did he bend over his victim, and only bother to lift his head? He didn't touch Antoine's wrist, or his chest, to check if the boy was dead . . . He looked at his face . . .

To be sure that it really was the man he had decided to

kill? From that moment something was wrong. Why did he stab the man lying on the ground three more times?

It was a film that Maigret replayed constantly in his head, as if he was hoping that he would suddenly understand.

'Place de la Bastille,' he said to the taxi-driver.

The landlord of the Café des Amis was still at the till, with his hair combed over his bald patch. Their eyes met, and there was nothing affable about the café manager's expression. Rather than sit on the ground floor, Maigret went down to the basement, where he found a place at a table. There were many more people than in the morning. It was time for aperitifs. When the waiter came to take his order, he was less friendly than before.

'A beer, please.'

And, holding out a packet of photographs:

'See if you recognize one of these men.'

'I haven't got much time.'

'It'll only take you a moment.'

The manager must have had a word with him when he saw the inspector emerging from the basement after spending a lot of time down there.

The waiter hesitated, then took the photographs.

'I should go and look at them in the back room.'

He came back almost immediately and held out the bundle to Maigret.

'I don't recognize anybody.'

He seemed sincere and went to fetch the beer that Maigret had ordered. Maigret had nothing planned except going home for dinner. He drank his beer slowly, climbed the stairs to the ground floor and, just opposite, saw Lapointe sitting alone at a table.

Lapointe spotted him too but pretended not to know him. Émile Branchu must have been somewhere in the café, and Maigret preferred not to look too hard at the customers.

He had two hundred metres to walk to his apartment, which smelled of baked mackerel. Madame Maigret cooked them in white wine, on a low heat, with lots of mustard.

She understood straight away that he wasn't happy with his investigation and asked no questions.

At the table, she said:

'Don't you want the television on?'

It had become a habit, an obsession.

'They talked a lot about Antoine Batille on the seven o'clock news. They went to the Sorbonne to interview some of his fellow students.'

'And what did they say about him?'

'That he was well behaved, rather self-effacing, a little embarrassed at belonging to such a well-known family. He had a passion for tape recorders and was waiting for a miniature version that you can hold in the palm of your hand to arrive from Japan.'

'Is that all?'

'They tried to question his sister, who only replied:

' "I have nothing to say."

' "Where were you that night?"

' "In Saint-Germain-des-Prés."

' "Did you get on well with your brother?"

' "He minded his business and I minded mine." '

Journalists were rummaging everywhere: Rue Popincourt, Quai d'Anjou, at the Sorbonne. Police stations on
the edge of the city were getting involved. They had
already found a label for the crime: 'The lunatic of Rue
Popincourt'.

They stressed the number of stab wounds: seven! In
two rounds! The murderer had retraced his steps, as if he
hadn't finished, to strike again.

Doesn't that suggest the idea of revenge [one of the
reporters insinuated]? If the seven knife blows had been
delivered one after the other, this might plausibly be a
case of crazed, unpremeditated rage. Juries always inter-
pret multiple blows as the sign of a murderer who has
lost control. Batille's murderer walked away, then calmly
retraced his steps to deliver the last three blows.

One of the papers ended with:

Did the tape recorder play a part in this case? We believe
that the police attach a certain importance to it, but
nobody at Quai des Orfèvres has agreed to answer questions on the subject.

At 8.30, the phone rang.

'This is Neveu, chief. Lucas suggested I should keep you
up to date.'

'Where are you?'

'In the little bar opposite the framing shop. Before Lourtie and I got there, Émile Branchu closed his door and

walked in the direction of Place de la Bastille, where he had an aperitif. As he passed the till he greeted the manager, who returned his greeting as if he was a local.

'The framer didn't talk to anyone, he just read the papers he had in his pocket. Lapointe was—'

'I saw.'

'Fine. Do you also know that he went for dinner in a modest restaurant where they keep a napkin for him and call him Monsieur Émile?'

'I didn't know that.'

'Lapointe claims to have eaten very well there. Apparently the *andouillette* . . .'

'And then?'

'Branchu came home, closed the shutter of the shop and attached the wooden panel over the glass door. There's a faint light coming through the slats of the shutters. Lourtie is watching the courtyard.'

'Do you have a car?'

'It's parked a few metres from here.'

On the first channel, male and female singers were prancing about. Maigret hated that kind of thing. On the second channel there was an old American film with Gary Cooper, which Maigret and his wife watched.

The film finished at 10.45, and Maigret was brushing his teeth, in his shirt-sleeves, when the phone rang again. This time it was Lourtie.

'Where are you?' Maigret asked him.

'Rue Fontaine. The framer went out at about ten thirty, and went and got his car from the courtyard. Neveu and I took the police car.'

'He didn't notice that you were following him?'

'I don't think so. He came right here, as if he had done so many times, and after finding a place to park he went inside the Lapin Rose.'

'What's the Lapin Rose?'

'A strip club. The doorman greeted him as if he knew him. We went in as well, Neveu and I, because in those places two men attract less attention than one on his own. Neveu even pretended to be slightly drunk.'

That was Neveu, who loved adding a personal touch. He also liked disguises, which he perfected down to the tiniest details.

'Our man is at the bar. He's shaken hands with the barman. The manager, a little fat man in a dinner-jacket, came and shook his hand too, and two or three of the girls kissed him.'

'What about the barman?'

'I was coming to that. He looks very much like the description we were given. Between thirty and forty. Good-looking guy, Mediterranean type.'

Leaving the Café des Amis, Maigret should have handed the bundle of photographs back to Lucas, who was still in Rue du Faubourg-Saint-Antoine, to pass on to Lourtie. He had thought about it when leaving Quai des Orfèvres, then it slipped his mind.

'Go back to the Lapin Rose. I'll be up there in twenty minutes. What's the name of the bar you're calling me from?'

'You can't miss it. It's the local café. I didn't want to call from the club for fear that I might be heard.'

'Be at the bar in twenty minutes.'

Madame Maigret had understood and, with a sigh, she went and fetched her husband's overcoat and hat from their hooks.

'Shall I call a taxi?'

'Thank you. Yes.'

'Will you be long?'

'Less than an hour.'

Even though they had had a car for a year – which Maigret had never driven – Madame Maigret preferred to use it as little as possible in Paris. They used it mostly, on Saturday evening or Sunday morning, to go to Meung-sur-Loire, where they had their weekend home.

'When I retire . . .'

Sometimes it seemed as if Maigret was counting the days until he could step down. Other times he appeared to be panicking at the prospect of leaving Quai des Orfèvres.

Until three months before, retirement age for detective inspectors was sixty-five, and he was sixty-three. A new decree had just changed everything, and moved the age to sixty-eight.

In some streets, the fog was thicker than in others, and the cars drove slowly, with a halo around their headlights.

'I've driven you before, haven't I?'

'That's entirely possible.'

'That's funny, I can't put a name to your face. I know you're well known. An actor?'

'No.'

'You've never been in films?'

'No.'

'And I haven't seen you on television?'

Luckily they reached Rue Fontaine.

'Try to find a place to park and wait for me.'

'Will you be long?'

'A few minutes.'

'Then that's fine. Because people will be coming out of the theatres and . . .'

Maigret opened the door to the bistro and found Lourtie leaning on the bar. He ordered a cognac, because they'd been talking a lot about cognac the day before, then took the photographs out of his pocket and slipped them into Lourtie's hand.

'Go and look at them in the toilet, it'll be safer.'

A few minutes later, Lourtie returned and handed the photographs back to the inspector.

'He's the one on top of the bundle. I've drawn a cross on the back.'

'There's no possible doubt?'

'None. Just that he's three or four years younger in the photograph. He's still a handsome fellow.'

'Go back down there.'

'The stripping's about to start. We had to order champagne. It's the only thing they serve.'

'Go on. And if something happens, particularly if the framer leaves town, don't hesitate to call me.'

In the taxi he looked at the photograph marked with a cross. He was the handsomest man in the packet. There was something stubborn and sarcastic about his face. A hard man, the kind you come across in gangs from Corsica or Marseille.

Maigret had a troubled night's sleep. He reached head-quarters before nine o'clock and sent Janvier up to Records.

'Any luck? I didn't dare to hope so. The instruction was quite vague.'

Janvier came down a quarter of an hour later with a file.

Mila, Julien Joseph François, born in Marseille, barman. Single. Height . . .

After this came the various measurements of the man called Mila whose last known address was a boarding house in Rue Notre-Dame-de-Lorette.

Sentenced four years earlier to two years in prison for involvement in an armed robbery. It happened at the entrance to a factory in Puteaux. The attacker had released the spring of his briefcase, from which thick smoke had emerged. A constable at the crossroads had noticed. A chase. The robbers' car had crashed into a streetlamp.

Mila had got off lightly, first of all because he had claimed to be only a decoy, and then because the criminals had used toy guns.

Maigret sighed. He knew professionals very well but he had never been very interested in them. For him it was routine, a kind of game with its own rules, and sometimes its ruses and tricks.

Was it likely that a man who had used a toy gun in a hold-up would have attacked a young man twice, just because he had recorded scraps of a compromising conversation? Or that once the young man had been killed, the murderer hadn't taken the trouble to take his tape recorder or make it unusable?

'Hello. Put me through to Poiret, the examining magistrate, please . . . Hello, yes . . . Thank you . . . Monsieur Poiret? Maigret speaking. I have some information here that raises a number of questions and I'd like to pass it to you . . . Half an hour? Thank you. I'll be at your office in half an hour.'

All of a sudden it was sunny. It was as if spring had turned up as arranged on 21 March. Maigret, with the photograph of Mila in his pocket, went to the commissioner's office for the briefing, as he did every morning.

It was a day of comings and goings, of phone calls, of setting things up. The little gang, of which so far they knew only Mila and the framer, plus a third person as yet unidentified, was apparently planning a burglary in a country house near Paris.

However, once it was beyond the boundaries of Paris, the Police Judiciaire of Quai des Orfèvres became powerless. This was the domain of Sûreté Nationale in Rue des Saussaies and, with the agreement of the examining magistrate, Maigret called his counterpart there.

This was Detective Chief Inspector Grosjean, a veteran who was more or less the same age as Maigret and who, like him, always had a pipe in his mouth. He was originally from Cantal, and still had the delightful accent.

They met a little later in the huge buildings in Rue des Saussaies that the people from the Police Judiciaire liked to call 'the factory'.

After an hour's work, Grosjean got to his feet, grumbling:

'I'll still have to pretend to report this to my boss.'

By the time Maigret got back to his office, everything had been organized. Not necessarily as he would have liked, but the way Sûreté Nationale usually worked.

'So?' asked Janvier, who had stayed in contact with the men carrying out the stakeout in Rue du Faubourg-Saint-Antoine.

'What a circus!'

'Lucas and Marette are at Rue du Faubourg-Saint-Antoine. Émile came for an aperitif at the bar where they were based, without paying them any attention. Then he went for lunch in the same restaurant as the previous night.

'No comings and goings. Two or three customers who look like real customers. There's a little studio that communicates with the shop, and that's where he does his tinkering.'

At about four o'clock, Maigret had to go back up to see the magistrate to keep him up to date on the plan of action they had undertaken. When he came back down, he was handed a form on which only a name had been written, leaving blank the space reserved for the purpose of the visit: *Monique Batille.*

How had her first name turned from Monique to Minou? He headed towards the waiting room and saw a tall, thin girl wearing dark trousers and a trenchcoat over a see-through blouse.

'You're Detective Chief Inspector Maigret, isn't that right?'

She seemed to look him up and down to check that he was worthy of his reputation.

'If you would be so kind as to follow me.'

Without a hint of awkwardness she went into that office where so many fates had been played out. Seemingly oblivious, she remained casual and took a pack of Gitanes out of her pocket.

'Is it OK to smoke?'

A chuckle.

'I forgot that you smoke your pipe all day!'

She walked to the window.

'It's like where we live. You can see the Seine. Don't you think it gets boring?'

What did she want, moveable scenery?

At last she slumped into the armchair while Maigret went on standing by his desk.

'You must be wondering why I've come here. Don't worry: I'm not here out of simple curiosity. I must confess that while I associate with all kinds of celebrities, I've never met a policeman before.'

There was no point in trying to interrupt her. Was it a mask she wore to conceal a deep shyness?

'Yesterday, I expected you to come and question my parents again, and question me and then the servants, what do I know. Isn't that what usually happens? This morning I decided I'd come and see you in the afternoon. I've been thinking a lot . . .'

She spotted the faint smile on Maigret's lips and guessed what was on his mind.

'I do think sometimes, believe me. I don't just say the

first thing that comes into my head. My brother's body was found in Rue Popincourt. It's not an awful street, is it?'

'What would you call an awful street?'

'A street where thugs meet up in bars and plan their evil deeds, I don't know . . .'

'No. It's just a street where ordinary people live.'

'I thought so. Well, my brother went and did his recordings in other places, really dangerous places. Once I insisted that he take me along, and he said:

' "Out of the question, little girl. You wouldn't be safe in the places I go to. I'm not safe there either."

'I asked him:

' "You mean there are criminals there?"

' "Definitely. Do you know how many bodies are fished out of the Canal Saint-Martin alone every year?"

'I don't think he was trying to scare me, or get rid of me. I insisted. I tried again several times, but he never wanted to take me along on what he called his expeditions.'

Maigret looked at her, surprised that she was nonetheless a sweet girl beneath her studied, sophisticated exterior. And fundamentally her brother seemed, like her, to have been nothing but a big child.

On the pretext of carrying out psychological research, documenting humanity, in a sense he was trying to frighten himself.

'Did he keep the recordings?'

'There are dozens of cassettes in his room, carefully numbered to match a catalogue that he regularly updated.'

'Has anyone touched them since . . . since he died?'

'No.'

'Is the body at your home?'

'The little drawing room, the one that we call Mother's drawing room, has been turned into a chapel of rest. The other drawing room is too big. There are also black curtains over the door of the building. It's all very gloomy. That sort of thing shouldn't exist these days, don't you think?'

'What else do you want to tell me?'

'Nothing. That he took risks. That he met all kinds of people. I don't know if he talked to them, or if he had contacts in those circles.'

'Did he ever carry a weapon?'

'It's funny that you should ask me that.'

'Why?'

'He persuaded our father to give him one of his revolvers. He kept it in his room. And not long ago he said to me:

' "I'm so happy that I've just turned twenty one. I'm going to apply for a firearms licence. Given the nature of the kind of research I'm carrying out . . ." '

This gave the scene in Rue Popincourt a new sense of drama, while at the same time making it seem almost unreal. A big kid. He was convinced that he was studying humans in their natural habitat, in bars and restaurants, he recorded scraps of conversation. He carefully labelled his findings when he filled in his catalogue.

'I'll need to listen to those recordings. Have you ever heard them?'

'He never let anyone hear them. Only one day I thought I heard a woman sobbing in his room. I went to see. He was on his own, listening to his tapes. Is there anything else you want to ask me?'

'Not right now. I'll probably call in at your apartment tomorrow during the day. I suppose a lot of people are passing through?'

'It doesn't stop all day. Well, there we are. I hoped I could be useful to you.'

'You may be even more useful than you think. Thank you for coming.'

He walked her to the door and held out his hand. She was very happy.

'Good evening, Monsieur Maigret. Don't forget that you promised I'd be able to listen to the recordings with you.'

He hadn't promised anything at all, but he preferred not to argue.

What had he been doing when he found her visitor form in his office? He had just come down from the examining magistrate's office.

'A circus,' he thought grumpily.

And he remained grumpy all evening and for much of the night. Because it really was a circus, the kind they know how to organize in Rue des Saussaies.

At 7.30, Lucas phoned to say that the framer had lowered his shutters and attached the panel to the glass door. A little later he went to his usual restaurant for dinner. Then he went for a walk as if to get some fresh air, all the way to Bastille, where he bought several magazines from the kiosk, and then went home.

'What should we do?'

'Wait.'

Maigret and Janvier went for dinner at the Brasserie

Dauphine. There was hardly anyone there. The two little rooms were particularly full at midday and around the evening aperitif.

Maigret called his wife to say hello.

'I have no idea what time I'll be back. It will probably be late. Unless somebody messes up. I'm not in charge of operations.'

He was only in charge of them in Paris, and that was why, at nine o'clock, the car in which he was sitting, with Janvier at the wheel and fat Lourtie in the back seat, pulled up just outside the framer's shop, or not far away.

It was a black car, without any distinctive markings, but it was fitted with a radio transmitter and receiver. Another car, exactly the same and similarly equipped, was parked about fifty metres away. It contained Detective Chief Inspector Grosjean and three of his inspectors.

Finally, in a sidestreet, there was a police van from Rue des Saussaies, with about ten plainclothes policemen inside.

Lucas was on guard, he too in a car, not far from Mila's furnished room in Rue Notre-Dame-de-Lorette.

He was the one who moved first.

'Hello . . . 287? . . . Is that you, chief?'

'This is Maigret.'

'Lucas speaking. Mila has just left in a taxi. We're passing through the centre of the city, and it seems we're going to be heading along the left bank.'

At the same time, the door to the shop opened, and the framer, who was wearing a beige, lightweight overcoat, locked the door and strode off towards Place de la Bastille.

'Hello . . . 215 . . .' Maigret called. 'Is that you, Grosjean? Do you read me? . . . Hello . . . 215 . . .'

'215 here.'

'We want to go slowly towards Bastille. He's on foot.'

'Over and out?'

'Over and out.'

Maigret shrugged heavily.

'To think that I'm playing a game of soldiers!'

At Place de la Bastille, Émile Branchu walked towards Boulevard Beaumarchais and opened the door of a parked black Citroën DS that immediately pulled away from the pavement.

Maigret couldn't see the man who was driving, probably the third man from the Café des Amis, the one who had been drinking rum, and who had a scar on his face.

Grosjean followed at a certain distance. He called from time to time, and Maigret replied, trying not to seem too bad-tempered. The van also stayed in contact.

There wasn't much traffic. The DS drove quickly, and the driver didn't seem to notice that he was being followed. More importantly, he didn't suspect that he was at the head of a little cortège.

At Porte de Châtillon, he stopped briefly, and a tall, dark-haired man standing by the pavement got into the car quite naturally.

Now all three of them were united. They too were organized with almost military precision. They speeded up, and Janvier was careful not to lose sight of them without making himself noticed.

They had taken the Versailles road and were passing through Petit Clamart almost without slowing down.

'Where are you?' Grosjean asked regularly. 'You're not losing sight of them?'

'We're leaving my territory,' Maigret grumbled. 'You're in charge from now on.'

'When we've reached our destination.'

They turned left towards Châtenay-Malabry, then to the right, towards Jouy-en-Josas. There were big clouds, some of them quite low, but much of the sky was clear, and the moon appeared from time to time.

The DS slowed down, turned left again, and shortly afterwards it could be heard braking.

'Shall I stop here?' Janvier asked. 'I think they're stopping. Yes. They've stopped.'

Lourtic got out of the car to go and see. When he came back, he announced:

'They've found someone who was waiting for them. They've gone into a big garden or park, I'm not sure, where you can see the roof of a villa.'

Grosjean, lost in the countryside, wondered where they were, and Maigret informed him.

'Where did you say you were?'

And Lourtie whispered:

'Chemin des Acacias. I saw the sign.'

'Chemin des Acacias . . .'

Lourtie had taken up position on the corner of the road where Mila and his companions had got out of the car. They had left the DS on the edge of the pavement. The lookout was still there, while the three others seemed to have entered the house.

The car from Rue des Saussaies pulled up behind Maigret's and then, a few moments later, the impressive van crammed full of police officers.

'Your turn now,' Maigret sighed, stuffing his pipe.

'Where are they?'

'Probably in the villa whose gate you can see on the corner. The man on the pavement is their lookout.'

'Are you not coming with me?'

'I'm staying here.'

A few minutes later Grosjean's car turned into the path on the left, so impetuously that the lookout, caught off guard, didn't have time to give the alarm. Before he knew what was happening, two men were on top of him and putting him in handcuffs.

From the van, the policemen dashed into the villa's garden and hurried to surround it, checking all the exit routes. It was a modern construction, very large, and the water that could be seen glittering behind the trees was the swimming pool.

All the windows were in darkness, the shutters closed. But then there was the sound of footsteps, and when, with Grosjean at their head, the men from Rue des Saussaies opened the door, they found in front of them three figures in rubber gloves who, alerted by suspicious sounds, were trying to flee.

They didn't insist, they put their arms in the air, without a word, and, a few moments later, they too had handcuffs on their wrists.

'Put them in the van. I'll question them as soon as I'm back in my office.'

Maigret took a short walk to stretch his legs. From a distance he watched the men being pushed into the van, and saw Grosjean coming towards him.

'Won't you come with me to take a look inside?'

First of all, they noticed, to the right of the gate, a pink marble plaque bearing the words, in gold letters: 'The Golden Crown'. A crown carved into the stone reminded Maigret of something. What? He couldn't remember.

There was no corridor. They stepped straight into a vast hall, where hunting trophies and paintings alternated on white stone walls. One of them had been unhooked and rested face-down on a mahogany table.

'A Cézanne,' Grosjean murmured after turning it the right way up.

There was a Louis XV desk in a corner. The leather desk blotter bore the same crown with, below it, a name: Philippe Lherbier.

'Come and look at this, Grosjean.'

He showed him the crown on the desk blotter, then the writing paper.

'Do you recognize it? The famous leather merchant in Rue Royale.'

A sixty-year-old man, with thick, immaculately white hair that made his face look fresher and younger.

Not only was the shop the most elegant leather merchant's in Paris, but it had branches in Cannes, Deauville, London, New York and Miami.

'What should I do? Should I give him a call?'

'That's up to you.'

He picked up the phone and dialled the number inscribed on the writing paper.

'Hello. Is this Monsieur Lherbier? Monsieur Philippe Lherbier, yes. He isn't at home. Do you know where I could get hold of him? I'm sorry. At Monsieur Legendre's office in Boulevard Saint-Germain. Do you have the number?'

He took the pencil out of his pocket and wrote the numbers down on the fine writing paper embellished with a crown.

'Thank you.'

Legendre, the lawyer, was also a Parisian society figure.

Maigret looked at the paintings, two more Cézannes, a Derain, a Sisley. He opened a door and found a smaller, more feminine drawing room, its walls covered with Bouton d'Or silk paper. It reminded him of Quai d'Anjou. He had found himself in the same world again, and the two men probably knew each other, if only from meeting in places that they both frequented.

Philippe Lherbier often appeared in the papers, particularly with reference to his marriages and divorces. He was called the most divorced man in France. Five times? Six times?

The strangest thing was that after each divorce he waited less than six months to get married again. And always to the same kind of woman! All but one of them, an actress, were models with long, supple bodies and a more or less fixed smile. It was as if he only married them to dress them in gorgeous clothes and make them play a purely decorative role.

'Yes. Thank you for putting me through . . . Hello! . . . Monsieur Lherbier? . . . This is Detective Inspector Grosjean, of the Sûreté Nationale . . . I'm in your villa, at Jouy-en-Josas . . . What am I doing there? . . . I've just arrested three burglars who were after your paintings.'

Grosjean, with his hand over the receiver, whispered to Maigret:

'He laughed.'

And, speaking normally:

'What's that you say? That you're insured? Fine. You're not coming this evening? I can't leave the door open and I have no way of closing it. That means that one of my men will have to stay in the villa until you send someone, with a locksmith . . . I would . . .'

He paused for a moment listening, his face very red.

'He's hung up,' he murmured at last.

He was so furious that he had trouble breathing.

'Those are the people . . . the people . . .'

He probably wanted to add:

'. . . we risk our lives for . . .'

But he realized that in the end it would seem redundant at the very least.

'I don't know if he was involved, but he seemed to consider this business to be a happy joke.'

He instructed one of his men to stay in the villa until new orders were issued.

'Are you coming, Maigret?'

He still couldn't get over it.

'Paintings by Cézanne . . . By . . . It doesn't matter . . . Hundreds of thousands of francs' worth of paintings in a villa where you only ever go to spend the weekend . . .'

'He has a much bigger villa at Cap d'Antibes. It's also called the Golden Crown. If the papers are to be believed, he marks his cigars and cigarettes with the same gold crown. His yacht is called *The Golden Crown*.'

'Is that true?' Grosjean sighed in disbelief.

'Apparently so.'

'And no one makes fun of him?'

'That's up to whoever gets an invitation to one of his residences.'

They found themselves outside and stopped for a moment to look at the swimming pool, which must have been heated because a light steam rose from it.

'Will you come to Rue des Saussaies?'

'No. The burglary has nothing to do with me, because it didn't happen in my territory. I'd just like, tomorrow if possible, to question them about something else. I think Poiret, the examining magistrate, would like to speak to them too.'

'The case in Rue Popincourt?'

'That's what put us on to them.'

'That's true, but . . .'

Standing near the cars, the two men shook hands, each nearly as stout as the other, with the same careers, the same experiences behind them.

'I'm going to spend the rest of the night there . . . Ah well . . .'

Maigret sat down beside Janvier. Lourtie, on the back seat, smoked his cigarette, which appeared as a small red dot.

'And here we are, boys! So far, we've only been working for Rue des Saussaies. Tomorrow we'll try to work for us.'

And Janvier asked him, alluding to the less than cordial relations that had always existed between the two police bodies:

'Do you think they'll lend them to us?'

4.

It must have been a busy night at Rue des Saussaies, where journalists and photographers, alerted as always by God knows who, soon came running and invading the corridors.

As he shaved, at 7.30, Maigret automatically turned on the radio. It was time for the news, and, as he expected, they were talking about the villa in Jouy-en-Josas and the famous millionaire Philippe Lherbier, the man with six wives and golden crowns.

> . . . Four men are in custody, but Detective Chief Inspector Grosjean remains convinced that none of them is the true head of the gang, the brains behind the operation. On the other hand, there are rumours that Detective Chief Inspector Maigret might intervene, not in the case of the theft of the paintings but with regard to another crime they may have committed. We are maintaining the greatest discretion on the subject.

It was also from the radio that he learned a detail: the three robbers and the lookout were unarmed.

By nine o'clock he was in his office and, just after the briefing, he called Grosjean at Rue des Saussaies.

'Have you been able to get some sleep?'

'Barely three hours. I wanted to question them straight away. None of them is budging. There's one in particular who's exasperating me. It's Julien Mila, the barman, the most intelligent of the three. When you ask him questions he looks at you stupidly and says in a soft voice:

' "Unfortunately I have nothing to say." '

'Didn't they ask for a lawyer to be present?'

'Of course they did. Monsieur Huet, inevitably. I'm expecting him this morning.'

'When will you be able to send me these fine fellows? Monsieur Poiret is waiting for them too.'

'At some point in the afternoon, I hope. I suppose he'll have to let me have them, because I don't expect to be spending long with them. The list of burglaries of the same kind committed around Paris over the past two years is a long one, twelve at least, and I'm sure they're responsible for most if not all of them. What about you? Rue Popincourt?'

'No news.'

'Do you think my customers had anything to do with it?'

'I don't know. One of the burglars, the little, broad-shouldered one with the scar on his cheek, was wearing a light raincoat with a belt, wasn't he? And a brown hat.'

'Demarle, yes. We're studying his police record. Apparently he's a hard case, and he's been in trouble with the law on more than one occasion.'

'Branchu, known as Mimile? The framer?'

'No criminal record. He lived in Marseille for a long time, but he's originally from Roubaix.'

'I'll see you later.'

The newspapers published photographs of the criminals on the front page, handcuffs on their wrists, as well as a photograph of the leather merchant by the weighing station at Longchamps, in tails and a light-grey top hat.

Mila stared at the camera with an ironic smile. Demarle, the sailor with the scar, seemed quite surprised by what was happening to him, while the framer held his hands in front of his face. The lookout, poorly dressed in a suit that was too big for him, looked like a lowly stooge.

After an investigation that Detective Chief Inspector Grosjean of the Sûreté Nationale has been leading for almost two years, a good haul . . .

Maigret shrugged. He was thinking not so much about the crooks but, in spite of himself, about Antoine Batille. Almost always, he had often repeated, it was by getting to know the victim that one was led to his murderer.

The sun was pale. The sky was a very light blue. The temperature was still two or three degrees, and most of France was freezing, except the west coast.

He put on his coat, picked up his hat and called in at the inspectors' office.

'I'm going out for an hour or so, boys.'

Alone, for once. He wanted to go to Quai d'Anjou by himself. He went on foot, walking along the embankments to Pont Marie, which he crossed. He smoked his pipe slowly and kept his hands plunged in his pockets.

Once again his thoughts turned to the journey that the young man with the tape recorder had made that night, the night of 18 to 19 March, which was to be his last one.

Even from a distance he could see the black drapes that framed the coach-gate, with an enormous *B*, fringes and silver droplets. Passing in front of the lodge, he noticed the concierge following the comings and goings.

She was still young and attractive. Her black dress was brightened by a white collar and trimmings which made it look like a uniform. He hesitated about going into the lodge for no reason, because he wasn't looking for anything in particular.

He thought better of it and took the lift. The Batilles' door was on the latch. He pushed it open and walked to the little drawing room that had been turned into a chapel of rest. A very dignified old lady stood by the door and nodded to him. Was she a relative? A friend or a governess who represented the family?

A man, standing up, held his hat in front of him and moved his lips, reciting a prayer. A woman, who must have been a local shopkeeper, knelt on a prie-dieu.

Antoine hadn't yet been placed in his coffin, but was lying on the mortuary cot, his clasped hands wrapped in a rosary.

By the dancing candlelight, his face looked very young. He looked more like fifteen than twenty-one. Not only had he been shaved, but his long hair had been cut, probably so that those who filed past didn't take him for a hippie.

Maigret too mechanically moved his lips without

conviction, then returned to the entrance hall and looked for someone to speak to. He found a valet in a striped waistcoat vacuuming in the big drawing room.

'I'd like to see Mademoiselle Batille,' he said. 'Detective Chief Inspector Maigret.'

The valet hesitated and finally walked away, grumbling:

'If she's got up!'

She had, but she seemed not to be ready because he had to wait a good ten minutes and, when she appeared, she was in a dressing gown, her feet bare in her slippers.

'Have you found anything?'

'No. I would just like to visit your brother's bedroom.'

'I'm sorry for receiving you like this, but I slept very badly, and in any case I don't usually get up early.'

'Is your father here?'

'No. He had to go to the office. My mother is in her apartment, but I haven't seen her this morning. Come with me.'

They walked along a corridor, then another that crossed it at right angles. Passing through an open door, beyond which Maigret could see an unmade bed and a breakfast tray, she explained:

'That's my bedroom. Ignore it. It's a mess.'

Two doors further on was Antoine's bedroom, overlooking the courtyard, which received the oblique rays of the sun. The Scandinavian furniture was simple and harmonious. One wall was covered with shelves full of books, records and, on two of the shelves, cassette tapes.

On the desk there were books, notebooks, coloured

pencils and, in a glass bowl, three tiny turtles swimming in two centimetres of water.

'Did your brother like animals?'

'He'd moved on a bit. There was a time when he brought back all kinds of animals, a crow with a broken wing, for example, hamsters, white mice, a grass snake more than a metre long. He claimed that he tamed them, but he never did.'

There was also an enormous globe on a stand, a flute on a pedestal table and musical scores.

'Did he play the flute?'

'He took five or six lessons. There must be an electric guitar somewhere. He took piano lessons.'

Maigret smiled.

'Not for long, I suppose?'

'Nothing ever lasted for long.'

'Except his tape recorder.'

'That's true. That passion lasted for almost a year.'

'Did he have an idea of what he wanted to do in the future?'

'No. Or at least he didn't talk to anyone about it. Father would have liked him to sign up for the Science Faculty and do chemistry, so that he could take over the company, etcetera.'

'He didn't agree?'

'He hated business. I think he was ashamed of being the son of Mylène Perfumes.'

'What about you?'

'I don't care either way.'

It was pleasant in this room, among objects that were

different, certainly, but which felt like familiar objects. Someone had spent a lot of time in that room, and made it his kingdom.

Maigret picked up one of the cassettes from the shelf, but on the label there was only a number.

'His notebook, which he used as a catalogue, must be here,' Minou said. 'Wait.'

'Hang on. I imagine it must be up to date, because he was very serious about it.'

It was a simple school exercise book with squared pages. On the cover, Antoine had written in fancy letters, with pencils in several colours:

My experiments

It started with:

Cassette 1: Family at the dinner table one Sunday.

'Why one Sunday?' he asked.

'Because on the other days my father rarely comes home for lunch. And in the evening, he and my mother often go into town for dinner, or have guests over.'

Even so, he had devoted his first recording to the family.

Cassette 2: Autoroute du Sud one Saturday evening.
Cassette 3: Fontainebleau Forest at night.
Cassette 4: Métro 8 o'clock in the evening.
Cassette 5: Midday, Place de l'Opéra.

Then came the interval at the Théâtre du Gymnase, then the sounds of a self-service restaurant on Rue de Ponthieu, the drugstore on the Champs-Élysées.

Cassette 10: A café in Puteaux.

His curiosity widened, and very gradually changed social class: workers leaving the factory, accordions on Rue de Lappe, a bar in Rue des Gravilliers, the area around Canal Saint-Martin, the Bal des Fleurs at La Villette, a café in Saint-Denis.

It was no longer the centre of Paris that he was interested in, but the periphery, and one of the addresses was on the edge of a slum.

'Is it true that it was dangerous?'

'More or less. Let's say that it wasn't to be recommended, and he was right not to bring you along. The people who frequent such places don't like people poking their noses into their business, particularly not with a tape recorder.'

'You think it was because of that.'

'I don't know. I have my doubts. In order to be certain, I would need to have heard all the tapes. From what I can tell it would take hours, if not several days.'

'Are you not going to do that?'

'If I could take them away temporarily, I would give one of my inspectors the task of—'

'I don't dare to assume that responsibility. Since he died, my brother has become someone sacred, and everything that belonged to him has been given a new value, do you understand? Before, we used to treat him a little like a big kid, which sent him into a fury. It's true that in some senses he did stay very young.'

Maigret's eye wandered along the wall to photographs of nudes cut from an American magazine.

'That's very young too,' she broke in. 'I'm sure that my brother had never slept with a girl. He courted two or three of my friends, without ever going all the way.'

'Did he have a car?'

'My parents gave him a little English car for his twentieth birthday. For two months he spent his free time in the countryside and fitted the car with every imaginable accessory. Afterwards he lost interest in it, and only ever took it out when he really needed it.'

'Not for his night-time expeditions?'

'Never. I'll ask Mother if I can let you have the cassettes. I hope she's got up.'

It was 10.30. She went away for quite a long time.

'She trusts you,' she announced when she came back. 'All she asks is that you catch the murderer. My father, I should add in passing, is even more devastated than she is. He was his only son. Since it happened, he hasn't said a word to us, and he goes to his office early in the morning. How are we going to wrap all this up? We would need a suitcase, or a big cardboard box. A suitcase would be better. Wait. I think I know where to find what we need.'

The suitcase she brought a little later bore the gilded crown of the leather merchant in Rue Royale.

'Do you know Philippe Lherbier?'

'My parents know him. They've been to his house for

dinner two or three times, but he's not what you would call a friend. He's the man who spends his time getting divorced, isn't that right?'

'His country house was nearly burgled last night. Don't you listen to the radio?'

'Only on the beach, when it's playing music.'

She helped him put the cassettes in the suitcase, then added the notebook that served as a catalogue.

'Don't you have any more questions to ask me? You can always come and question me, and I promise to answer you as frankly as I have done so far.'

She was visibly excited to be helping the police.

'I won't walk you back to the door, because I'm not dressed to walk past the mortuary room. People would see it as a lack of respect. Why do we suddenly have to respect someone when they're dead, when you were dismissive of them when they were alive?'

Maigret left, a little encumbered by his suitcase, particularly when he passed in front of the concierge. He was lucky enough to see a woman getting out of a taxi and paying the driver, so he didn't have to wait to find one.

'Quai des Orfèvres.'

He wondered who to entrust with the recordings of Antoine Batille. He needed someone with a good knowledge of the places where the recordings were made, and who was familiar with the people who frequented them.

Eventually he went to the end of the corridor to find his colleague in the Vice Squad.

Since he was holding his suitcase, his colleague asked him ironically:

'Have you come to say goodbye before moving house?'

'I have some recordings here, most of them taken on the edge of Paris, in dance halls, cafés and bistros.'

'Am I supposed to be interested in that?'

'Maybe not, but I am, and it may have something to do with an ongoing case.'

'The one in Rue Popincourt?'

'Between ourselves, yes. I'd rather no one knew. One of your men must know these places, and perhaps the recordings will mean something to him.'

'I understand. Spotting a dangerous individual, for example. Somebody who, for fear of being compromised . . .'

'That's it exactly.'

'Old Mangeot. He's been in the job for almost forty years. He knows the fauna of those places better than anybody.'

He wasn't a stranger to Maigret.

'Has he got any free time?'

'I'll see to it that he does.'

'Does he know how to use those contraptions? I'll go and get the tape recorder from my office.'

When he came back, a sad man with soft features and dull eyes was standing in the office of the head of the Vice Squad.

He was one of the low-wage-earners in the Police Judiciaire, one of the men who, for want of a certain basic training, remain at the bottom of the heap for their whole lives. By dint of walking around Paris, they acquire the posture of butlers and café waiters who stand up all day. They almost assume the same dull colour as the impoverished areas that they patrol.

'I know these machines,' he said immediately. 'Are there a lot of cassettes?'

'About fifty. Maybe a few more.'

'At half an hour per cassette. Is it urgent?'

'Quite urgent.'

'I'll give him an office where he won't be disturbed,' the head of the Vice Squad broke in.

They explained in detail to Mangeot what was expected of him; he nodded to show that he had understood and went off with the suitcase while Maigret's colleague said in an undertone:

'Don't worry. He looks soft in the head. He definitely has no illusions, but he's still one of my most precious collaborators. A kind of hunting dog. We let him sniff a trail, and off he goes, head down.'

Maigret went back to his office, and he hadn't been there for ten minutes before the examining magistrate called him.

'I've tried to get through to you several times. First of all, congratulations on last night's haul.'

'Rue des Saussaies did all that.'

'I went to see the prosecutor, who is delighted. They're bringing me the four young men at three o'clock this afternoon. I'd like you to be in my office, because you know the case better than I do. When we've dealt with the burglaries, if you think it's useful you can bring them down to your office. I know you have a special way of carrying out your interrogations.'

'Thank you. I'll be in your office at three o'clock.'

He opened the door to the inspectors' office.

'Are you free for lunch, Janvier?'

'Yes, chief. I'll finish my report and . . .'

There were always reports, there was always paper-work.

'What about you, Lapointe?'

'You know I'm always free.'

Because that meant that all three of them were going to go for lunch in the Brasserie Dauphine.

'We'll meet at twelve thirty.'

Maigret didn't forget to call his wife, and she asked him as usual:

'Do you think you'll be back for dinner? A shame about lunch. I had snails.'

As if by chance, every time he didn't come back for a meal it was something of which he was particularly fond.

But perhaps they had snails at the Brasserie Dauphine as well . . .

At three o'clock, when Maigret stepped into the long corridor with the offices of the examining magistrates on either side, the flashes of the photographers went off as a dozen journalists came charging towards him.

'Are you coming to interrogate the gangsters?'

He tried to dodge them without giving an answer either way.

'Why are you here, and not Detective Chief Inspector Grosjean?'

'Goodness, I have no idea. Ask the examining magistrate.'

'You're the one in charge of the Rue Popincourt case, aren't you?'

He had no reason to deny it.

'Might there by any chance be a connection between the two cases?'

'Gentlemen, I have no statement to make for now.'

'You won't answer no?'

'You would be wrong to draw any conclusions.'

'You were in Jouy-en-Josas last night, isn't that right?'

'I won't deny it.'

'In what capacity?'

'My colleague Grosjean will be able to give you a more authoritative answer than I can.'

'Was it your men who discovered the trail of the thieves in Paris?'

The four men arrested the previous night were sitting on two benches on either side of the magistrate's door, handcuffs around their wrists, surrounded by gendarmes, and they were not unamused by the scene.

A short but bulky lawyer appeared from the far end of the corridor, his gown flapping like wings. Noticing the inspector, he walked towards him and shook his hand.

'How are things, Maigret?'

A flash. The handshake had been photographed, as if the whole scene had been prepared in advance.

'So what brings you here?'

Monsieur Huet asked that question in front of the journalists, and not by chance. He was skilful and quick-witted and was in the habit of defending high-level members of the underworld. Very cultured, a lover of music and theatre, he attended every dress rehearsal and major concert.

'What's keeping us from going in?'

'I don't know,' Maigret replied, not without irony.

And the little man with the broad shoulders knocked at the magistrate's door, opened it and gestured to Maigret to come in with him.

'Hello, my dear judge. I hope you're not too disappointed to see me here? My clients . . .'

The magistrate shook the lawyer's hand, and Maigret's.

'Take a seat, gentlemen. I will bring in the accused. I imagine that you aren't afraid of them, and that I can leave the gendarmes outside.'

He had the handcuffs removed. The rather cramped office was full. The clerk stood at one end of the table that served as a desk. An extra chair had to be brought from a storeroom. The four men stood on either side of their lawyer, and Maigret had sat down slightly apart from the others, in the background.

'First of all, as you know, I must identify the accused. You are each to respond when your name is called out. Julien Mila . . .'

'Here.'

'Your surname, first names, current address, place and date of birth, profession . . .'

'Milat with a *t*?' asked the clerk, who was writing.

'With an *a*, nothing more.'

It went on for quite a long time. Demarle, the man with the scar and the biceps of a fairground wrestler, was born in Quimper. He had been a sailor, and for now he was registered unemployed.

'Your address?'

'Here and there. I always find a friend to put me up.'

'In other words, you're homeless?'

'With what we got on unemployment benefit, you know . . .'

The fourth man, the lookout, was a poor, sickly-looking man who claimed to be an errand-boy and lived in Rue du Mont-Cenis, in Montmartre.

'How long have you been part of the gang?'

'Excuse me, your honour,' Huet cut in. 'First of all, we have to establish that there is indeed a gang.'

'I was just about to ask you a question. Which of these men do you represent?'

'All four of them.'

'Don't you think that during the preliminary hearing a conflict might arise between them as the result of a divergence of interests?'

'I severely doubt it, and if it did happen, I would call on my colleagues. Do you agree, gentlemen?'

All four of them nodded.

'Since we're still asking the preliminary questions, I was about to ask questions about ethical matters,' Huet continued with an ominous smile. 'You should be aware that since this morning this case has aroused a great deal of interest in the press. I've received quite a large number of phone calls, in the course of which I have collected information that has left me surprised, if not indeed shocked.'

He leaned back and lit a cigarette. The magistrate, faced with this prince of the bar, couldn't help feeling nervous.

'I'm listening.'

'The arrest, in fact, was not carried out in the usual style of apprehensions of this kind. Three radio cars, including a van full of plainclothes inspectors, arrived on the scene at more or less the same time as my clients, as if the police were aware of what was going to happen. And yet taking his place at the head of this procession was Detective Chief Inspector Maigret here, and two of his colleagues. Is that correct, Detective Chief Inspector?'

'It is correct.'

'I see that my informant was not mistaken.'

Someone from Rue des Saussaies, probably, perhaps a clerk or a typist?

'I thought, I have always thought, that the territory of Quai des Orfèvres was limited to Paris. Let us say greater Paris, of which Jouy-en-Josas is not a part.'

He had got what he wanted. He had taken control of operations, and the magistrate no longer knew how to reduce him to silence.

'Might it not be because the information about – shall we say this attempted burglary – came from the Police Judiciaire? You aren't answering, Maigret?'

'I have nothing to say.'

'Weren't you there?'

'I'm not here to be questioned.'

'However, I am going to ask you another more important question. Is it not the case that, while investigating a different case, also recent, you happened by chance upon this one?'

Maigret remained silent.

'Please, Monsieur Huet,' the magistrate cut in.

'Just one moment. Some inspectors from the Police Judiciaire have been identified to me as having mounted a stakeout, over the past two days, opposite Émile Branchu's shop. Detective Chief Inspector Maigret in person has been seen twice in a café in Bastille where my clients happened to meet the day before yesterday, and he questioned the waiters and tried to weasel out information from the manager. Is that correct? Forgive me, your honour, but I would like to put this case in its true perspective, which is perhaps not the one that you know.'

'Have you finished, Monsieur Huet?'

'For now.'

'Can I question the first of the accused? Julien Mila, please tell me who alerted you to Philippe Lherbier's villa, and who talked to you about the valuable paintings it contains.'

'I advise my client not to answer.'

'I'm not answering.'

'You are suspected of participating in the twenty-one burglaries of villas and chateaus which have taken place over the last two years in the same circumstances.'

'I have nothing to say.'

'All the more,' the lawyer cut in, 'in that you have no evidence.'

'I repeat my first question, extending it to the other cases. Who alerted you to these villas and chateaus? Who, then, probably the same person, took charge of the sale of the stolen paintings and artworks?'

'I don't know anything about any of that.'

The magistrate, with a sigh, turned his attention to the

framer, and Mimile proved no more talkative. As to Demarle the sailor, he was enjoying himself playing the clown.

The only one with a different attitude was the lookout, the one who was called Gouvion and who was of no fixed abode.

'I don't know what I'm doing here. I don't know these gentlemen. I found myself in the area in search of a place to kip that wasn't too cold.'

'Is that also your point of view, Monsieur Huet?'

'I agree with him completely, and I should point out that this man has no criminal record.'

'Does nobody have anything to add?'

'I would like to ask a question, at the risk of repeating myself. What is Detective Chief Inspector Maigret's role in this? And what will happen when we leave this office?'

'I am not obliged to reply.'

'Does that mean that another interrogation will take place, not at the Palais de Justice, but in the offices of the Police Judiciaire, to which I have no access? In other words, that it will involve not burglary, but another case entirely?'

'I apologize, Monsieur Huet, but I have nothing to tell you. You'll probably want to ask your clients to sign the provisional statement, which will be typed up, by tomorrow, in four copies.'

'You may sign them, gentlemen.'

'Thank you.'

And, rising to his feet, the examining magistrate walked towards the door, followed reluctantly by the lawyer.

'I must express my reservations . . .'

'I have noted them.'

Then, to the gendarmes:

'Please put the handcuffs back on the prisoners and take them to the Police Judiciaire. You can go through the communicating door. Would you stay for a moment, please, detective chief inspector?'

Maigret sat down again.

'What do you think?'

'I think that right now Monsieur Huet is busy informing the press and blowing this case out of proportion so that from tomorrow, perhaps even in this evening's final editions, it will be spread across two columns.'

'Does that bother you?'

'I wonder . . . Just now I would have said yes. My intention was to keep the two cases very separate from one another, and to make sure that the newspapers didn't get them mixed up. Now . . .'

He thought for a moment, weighing up the pros and cons.

'Perhaps it's better that way. By creating a stir, there is a chance that . . .'

'Do you think one of those four men . . . ?'

'I can't be certain of anything. Apparently a Swedish knife like the one used in Rue Popincourt was found in the sailor's pocket. The man wore a light raincoat with a belt and a brown hat. In any case, probably this evening, I'll put him in the presence of the Pagliatis, in the same street, in the same lighting, but it's hardly conclusive. The old lady on the first floor will also be called upon to identify him.'

'What are you hoping for?'

'I don't know. The burglaries are a matter for Rue des Saussaies. What interests me are the seven knife blows that cost a young man his life.'

When he came out of the magistrate's office, the journalists had disappeared, but he found them all, or perhaps even more, it seemed to him, in the corridor of the Police Judiciaire. The four suspects were nowhere to be seen, because they had been taken to an office, where they were being kept under close watch.

'What's happening, detective chief inspector?'

'Nothing out of the ordinary.'

'Are you dealing with the Jouy-en-Josas case?'

'You know very well that it has nothing to do with me.'

'Why are these four men here rather than having been driven back to Rue des Saussaies?'

'Well, let me tell you . . .'

He suddenly took a decision. Huet was bound to have talked to them about a connection between the two cases. Rather than seeing more or less precise and tendentious information, wasn't it better to tell the truth?

'Antoine Batille, gentlemen, had a passion: recording what he called living documents. With a tape recorder around his neck, he went to public spaces, to cafés, bars, dances, restaurants, even the Métro, and placed himself discreetly with his tape recorder turned on.

'On Tuesday evening, at about nine thirty, he was in a café on Place de la Bastille and, as usual, he had turned on his tape recorder. His neighbours were . . .'

'The burglars?'

'Three of them. The lookout wasn't there. The

recording isn't of the first order. Still, we can understand that a meeting is being arranged for two days later, and that a certain villa that has already been watched . . .

'Less than an hour later, in Rue Popincourt, the young man was attacked from behind and given seven stab wounds, one of which was fatal.'

'Do you think it was one of those men?'

'I don't think anything, gentlemen. My job is not to think, but to find evidence or obtain confessions.'

'Did anyone see the attacker?'

'Two passers-by, a certain distance away, and a lady who lives opposite the place where the murder was committed.'

'Do you think the burglars realized that their words had been recorded?'

'Once again, I don't think anything. It's a plausible hypothesis.'

'So Batille was followed by one of them until he was in quite a deserted place and . . . Did the murderer take the tape recorder?'

'No.'

'How do you explain that?'

'I don't explain it.'

'The passers-by that you mentioned . . . I assume they are the Pagliatis . . . You see, we know more than you might think . . . So did the Pagliatis, by rushing over, prevent the man from . . .'

'No. He had only delivered four blows. After leaving the scene he retraced his steps to deliver another three. So he could have pulled the tape recorder off the victim's neck.'

'So you haven't got anywhere?'

'I'm going to question those gentlemen.'

'Together?'

'One by one.'

'Who are you starting with?'

'Yvon Demarle, the sailor.'

'When will you have finished?'

'I don't know. You could leave one of your colleagues here.'

'And go for a beer! Good idea! Thanks, detective chief inspector.'

Maigret would also have liked to go for a beer. He went to his office and called in Lapointe, who knew how to do shorthand.

'Have a seat there. Take notes.'

Then, to Janvier:

'Will you go and fetch the man called Demarle?'

The ex-sailor turned up with his hands clasped in front of him.

'Take off the cuffs. And you, Demarle, take a seat.'

'What are you going to do to me? Give me the third degree? I should tell you straight out that I'm tough, and you're not going to get anything out of me.'

'Have you finished?'

'I wonder why, up there, I was allowed a lawyer while here I'm on my own.'

'Monsieur Huet will explain that when he sees you again. Among the objects taken from you was a Swedish knife . . .'

'And that's why you've brought me in? It's been hanging

about in my pocket for twenty years. It was a present from my brother, when I was still a fisherman in Quimper, before I started on the liners.'

'When did you last use it?'

'I use it every day to cut meat, the way you do in the country. It may not be elegant but . . .'

'On Tuesday evening, you were with two companions at the Café des Amis on Place de la Bastille.'

'That's what you say. You know, I can't remember what I did yesterday. They say I'm a bit absent-minded.'

'There was Mila, the framer and you. You spoke in more or less covert terms about the burglary, and among other things you were given the task of finding a car. Where did you steal it?'

'What?'

'The car.'

'What car?'

'I don't suppose you know where Rue Popincourt is either?'

'I'm not from Paris.'

'None of the three of you noticed a young man at the next table turning on a tape recorder?'

'A what?'

'You didn't follow that young man?'

'Why? Please don't think that's my kind of thing.'

'Your accomplices didn't tell you to gain possession of the cassette?'

'Right! It's a cassette now. Is that all?'

'That's all.'

And, to Janvier:

'Take him to the first free office. Same thing . . .'

Janvier was going to repeat the questions, more or less word for word. When he had finished, a third inspector would take over.

As it happened, Maigret didn't think much would come of it, but it was still the most efficient method. It could go on for hours. One such interrogation had lasted thirty-two hours before the man in question, who had come in as a witness, confessed to his crime. And yet, three or four times during the interrogation the police had been on the point of letting him go, he was so good at acting innocent.

'Go and get Mila for me,' he said to Lourtie in the inspectors' office.

The barman knew he was handsome, more intelligent, more alert than his accomplices. It was almost as if he enjoyed playing his part.

'Hang on! The chatterbox isn't here?'

He pretended to look around for his lawyer.

'Do you think it's normal practice to question me in his absence?'

'That's my business.'

'I'd just have to say that I wouldn't want the whole procedure to be declared irregular because of a detail.'

'What was your first conviction for?'

'I can't remember. Besides, you can find that out from Records upstairs. So even though I've never dealt with you personally, I have been a client here in the past.'

'When did you notice that your conversation was being recorded?'

'What conversation are you talking about, and what recording?'

Maigret was patient enough to take his questions to their conclusion, even though he knew it was pointless. And Lourtie would repeat them tirelessly, as Janvier was now doing with the sailor.

Then came the framer's turn. At first sight he seemed shy, but he was just as cool-headed as the others.

'Have you been burgling unoccupied villas for a long time?'

'I'm sorry?'

'I'm asking you if . . .'

Maigret was hot, and his back was sticky with sweat. The four men had agreed on a deal. Each one would play his part and avoid being caught off guard by more or less unexpected questions.

The sailor tramp stuck to his explanation. First of all, he wasn't at the meeting in Place de la Bastille. Then, on Tuesday night, he was looking for a 'crib', as he put it.

'In an unoccupied house?'

'As long as the door's open. In the house, or in the garage . . .'

At six in the evening, the four men were taken back in a police van to Rue des Saussaies, where they would spend the night.

'Is that you, Grosjean? Thanks for lending them to me . . . I didn't get anything out of them, no. They're not choir-boys.'

'You can say that again! We're all right with Tuesday's burglaries because they were caught red-handed. But as for the previous burglaries, if we don't find any evidence or witnesses . . .'

'When the papers get involved, witnesses will turn up, you'll see.'

'Do you still think that the crime in Rue Popincourt was committed by one of the four?'

'To tell you the truth, no.'

'Do you have any suspicions?'

'No.'

'So what are you planning to do?'

'Wait.'

And it was true. In their final edition the newspapers were already publishing the account of what had happened in the examining magistrates' corridor, and then the statements that Maigret had given at the Police Judiciaire.

Is this the Rue Popincourt murderer?

And below this question was the photograph of Yvon Demarle, handcuffs on his wrists, near Examining Magistrate Poiret's door.

Maigret looked for the telephone number of the apartment on Quai d'Anjou and dialled it.

'Hello, who's speaking?'

'Monsieur Batille's valet.'

'Is Monsieur Batille there?'

'He's not back yet. I think he had an appointment with his doctor.'

'This is Detective Chief Inspector Maigret. When is the funeral?'

'At ten o'clock tomorrow.'

'Thank you.'

Phew! Maigret's day was over, and he called his wife to say that he would be home for dinner.

'After which we'll go to the cinema,' he added.

To take his mind off things.

5.

Just by chance, Maigret was joined by young Lapointe. They were both standing in the crowd, on the embankment side, not opposite the dead boy's house but the house next door, because there were so many onlookers that they hadn't been able to find a better vantage point.

There were cars, including many chauffeur-driven limousines, all along the embankments, from Pont Louis-Philippe to Pont Sully, and others were parked on the other side of the island, on Quai de Béthune and Quai d'Orléans.

It was a cool morning, chilly, one might have said, very bright, very cheerful, pastel-coloured.

They saw the cars stopping in front of the big, black-draped gate, and people going inside and upstairs, where they would bow in front of the coffin before reappearing and waiting outside for the convoy to form.

A red-haired photographer, bare-headed, walked back and forth, pointing his lens at the rows of onlookers. He was not universally well received, and some people had no qualms about expressing their feelings to him.

Nonetheless, he carried on imperturbably with his work. The public, particularly the ones who complained, would probably have been surprised to learn that he didn't belong to a newspaper, an agency or a magazine, but that he was there on Maigret's orders.

Maigret had gone to the laboratory at the Police Judiciaire early that morning and, with Moers, had chosen Van
Hamme, the best and, most importantly, the most
resourceful of the available photographers.

'I would like photographs of all the onlookers, first of
all opposite the dead boy's house, then opposite the
church, when the coffin is brought there, then when it
comes out, and finally at the cemetery.

'Once the photographs have been developed, study
them under the magnifying glass. It's possible that one
person or several people will appear in all three places.
They're the ones who interest me. Make enlargements,
without the people around them.'

In spite of himself, Maigret looked around for a light-
coloured raincoat with a belt and a dark hat. There was
little chance of the murderer still wearing the same
clothes, because the morning papers had given a description of them. The two cases, the one in Rue Popincourt
and the burglary, were by now definitely seen as closely
connected.

There was much talk of the role of the Police Judiciaire
and the previous day's interrogations, and the photographs of the four arrested men had been published.

In one of the papers, below the portrait of Demarle the
sailor, in a raincoat and a brown hat, it said:

Is this the murderer?

The crowd was a mixture. First of all, near the house,
there were those who had gone to pay their last respects

to the dead boy, and who were waiting to take their place in the cortège. Along the pavement it was particularly the residents of the island, and the concierges and shopkeepers of Rue Saint-Louis-en-l'Ile.

'Such a nice boy! . . . And so shy! . . . When he came into the shop, he always raised his hat . . .'

'If only he had cut his hair a bit shorter . . . His parents should have told him . . . Elegant people like that . . . It made him look like a bad sort . . .'

Maigret and Lapointe exchanged a glance from time to time, and an absurd idea came into the former's mind. How eagerly Antoine Batille would have slipped around this crowd with his microphone if he had been alive! Although if he had been alive, there would have been no crowd.

The hearse appeared and pulled up at the kerb, followed by three more cars. Were they going to drive to the church of Saint-Louis-en-l'Ile, which was two hundred metres away?

The people from the funeral director's first of all took down the wreaths and bouquets. It wasn't only the hearse that was covered with them; flowers were also piled up in the three cars.

Among the people waiting there was a third category: standing in small groups, the staff of Mylène Perfumes. Many of the girls and young women were pretty, dressed with an elegance which, in the morning sun, had a somewhat aggressive quality.

There was a movement in the crowd, like a current passing from one end of the rows to the other, and the coffin appeared, carried by six men. Once it had been slid into the hearse, the family appeared. At its head, Gérard Batille was flanked by his wife and daughter. His features were very drawn, his complexion muddy. He didn't look at anyone but seemed surprised to discover so many flowers.

It was as if he wasn't fully present, as if he barely realized what was happening around him. Madame Batille showed greater composure, although she sometimes dabbed her eyes through the thin black veil that covered her face.

Minou, the sister, whom Maigret was seeing in black for the first time, seemed taller and thinner, and she was the only one who paid attention to what was going on around her.

Other photographers, these ones press cameramen, took some photographs. Aunts, uncles and more or less distant relatives followed, and also, in all likelihood, the senior staff of the perfume and beauty products company.

The hearse moved off, the cars full of flowers, and the family took their place behind it, then the friends, students, teachers, and finally the local shopkeepers.

Some of the onlookers headed towards Pont Marie or Pont Sully to go back to their jobs, but others set off towards the church.

Maigret and Lapointe were among them. They followed the procession along the pavement and, on Rue Saint-Louis-en-l'Ile, they found another crowd that hadn't been at Quai d'Anjou. The church was already more than half full. From the street they could hear the deep murmur of a pipe organ, and the coffin was carried to the bier, which was only partly covered by flowers.

A lot of people had stayed outside. The doors hadn't been closed again, and the absolution was already underway when the sun and the cool air entered the church.

'Pater Noster . . .'

The priest, who was very old, walked around the bier waving his sprinkler and then swung the censer.

'Et ne nos inducas in tentationem . . .'

'Amen.'

Outside, Van Hamme was still working.

'Which cemetery?' Lapointe asked under his breath, leaning over Maigret's shoulder.

'Montparnasse. The Batilles have a family vault there.'

'Are we going?'

'I don't think so.'

Luckily a lot of police officers had come to control the traffic. The immediate family took their seats in a car at the front. The more distant relations followed, then came Batille's colleagues and friends who ran to find their cars and tried to edge their way in.

Van Hamme had taken the precaution of getting a lift in a little black police car that was waiting at a strategic point and picked him up at the last moment.

The crowd gradually dispersed. Some groups were still conversing on the pavements.

'We can go back,' Maigret sighed.

They crossed the pedestrian bridge behind Notre Dame and stopped in a bar on the corner of Boulevard du Palais.

'What will you have?'

'A white wine. A Vouvray.'

Because the word Vouvray was written in chalk on the mirrors.

'Me too. Two Vouvrays.'

It was nearly midday when Van Hamme stepped into Maigret's office with some photographs.

'I haven't finished, but there was something I wanted to show you straight away. Three of us have been studying the photographs with a strong magnifying glass. I was immediately struck by this.'

The first photograph, on Quai d'Anjou, showed only part of the body and the face, because a woman was pushing from the side, trying to slip into the front row.

The man was incontestably wearing a lightweight beige raincoat and a dark hat. He was quite young, about thirty. His face was ordinary, and he seemed to be frowning as if displeased by something around him.

'Here's a slightly better photograph.'

The same face, enlarged. The mouth was quite thick, almost sulky, and the expression was that of a shy person.

'This is still Quai d'Anjou. We'll see if he's in the photographs taken in front of the church that we're developing right now. I brought these down to you because of the raincoat.'

'Weren't there any other raincoats?'

'Several, but only three with belts, one middle-aged man with a beard, and a man in his forties without a hat, smoking a pipe.'

'Bring down anything else you find after lunch.'

Basically, the raincoat didn't mean very much. If Batille's murderer had read the morning papers, he knew that they had published his description. Why, then, wear the same outfit as he had in the evening in Rue Popincourt? Because it was the only one he had? Out of defiance?

Maigret had lunch at the Brasserie Dauphine again, just with Lapointe this time, because Janvier and Lucas weren't in the building.

At 2.30, Maigret received a phone call that relaxed him. It was as if a large part of his worries evaporated all at once.

'Hello, Detective Chief Inspector Maigret? I'm putting you through to Monsieur Frémiet, our senior editor. Please stay on the line.'

'Hello . . . Maigret?'

The two men had known each other for a long time. Frémiet was the editor of one of the biggest morning newspapers.

'I'm just asking if your investigation is making any progress. I'm taking the liberty of calling you because we've just received quite a curious message. And it came by express telegram, which is quite rare for an anonymous communication . . .'

'I'm listening . . .'

'You know that we published the photograph of the members of the Jouy-en-Josas gang this morning. Below the picture of the sailor my editor insisted on printing the words "Is this the murderer?" '

'I saw.'

'This cutting that has just reached us has just one word written in green ink, in large letters: "No!" '

Maigret's face brightened.

'If you'll forgive me, I'm going to send one of my men to fetch the message. Do you know which post office it was sent from?'

'Rue du Faubourg-Montmartre. May I ask you, inspector, not to mention this to any other journalists. I can't publish this document until tomorrow morning. It's already been photographed, and the print will be ready shortly. Unless you ask us to keep it secret . . . ?'

'No. On the contrary. I'd even like you to comment on it. One moment. The best thing would be to suggest that it's a joke, stressing that the real murderer wouldn't risk compromising himself like that.'

'I think I understand.'

'Thank you, Frémiet. I'll send someone to you straight away.'

He went into the inspectors' office, sent one of them to the Champs-Élysées and asked Lapointe to follow him into his office.

'You look quite perky, chief.'

'Not really! Not really! There's still a chance that I may be mistaken.'

He told Lapointe the story of the photograph cut from the newspaper and the 'No!' written in green ink.

'I'm even quite pleased about this green ink.'

'Why?'

'Because the person who struck seven times, in two rounds, if one might put it like that, under lashing rain, while a couple was walking along the pavement and a woman was looking through the window, isn't entirely a man like any other.

'I've often noticed that people who use green ink, or red ink, feel a profound need to distinguish themselves. For them it's only one way of doing it.'

'Do you mean that he's a madman?'

'I wouldn't go that far. A lot of people would say: an oddball. They exist on various levels.'

Van Hamme stepped into the office, carrying a thick bundle of photographs, some of which were still wet.

'Have you found the man in the raincoat anywhere else?'

'Only three people apart from family and close friends appear in all three places: Quai d'Anjou, outside the church and finally not far from the vault, in Montparnasse Cemetery . . .'

'Show me.'

'First of all, there's this woman.'

A young woman of about twenty-five with a dramatic facial expression. She looked uneasy, tormented. She wore a badly cut black coat, and her hair fell untidily on either side of her face.

'You told me only to pay attention to the men, but I thought . . .'

'I understand.'

Maigret looked at her intensely, as if to penetrate her secret. She looked like a working-class girl who paid little attention to her outward appearance.

Why was she as upset as the members of the family, more upset than Minou, for example?

Minou had told him that her brother had probably never slept with a woman. Was she sure of that? Might she have been mistaken? And wasn't it possible that Antoine had a girlfriend?

In the state of mind revealed by his pursuit of human voices in the most working-class districts, might not a girl like that have been the kind to interest him?

'In a moment, Lapointe, when we have finished, go back to Ile Saint-Louis. I don't know why, but I can see her as a sales-girl in a grocer's shop, or a dairy, what do I know? Perhaps a waitress in a café or a restaurant.'

'The second individual,' Van Hamme announced, showing the enlarged photograph of a man in his fifties.

Had his clothes been slightly untidier, he might have been taken for a tramp. He looked straight ahead, with a resigned appearance, and one wondered why the funeral was interesting to him.

It was hard to imagine him stabbing a young man seven times and then running off. The murderer hadn't come to the area in a car, that was more or less certain. It was more likely that he had taken the Métro at Voltaire station, very close to the place where the crime had been committed. The Métro clerk had only confused memories, because six or seven people had arrived at the station entrance in the space of one or two minutes. He had been punching tickets without looking up. It was mechanical.

'If I were to look at everyone who came through, my

head would be spinning . . . Faces and more faces . . . Almost all of them grumpy . . .'

Why had this shabbily dressed man stayed in front of the house, and then in front of the church, and why had he gone to Montparnasse Cemetery after that?

'What about the third one?' Maigret asked.

'You know him. He's the one I showed you this morning. You'll notice that he doesn't hide. He must have noticed that I was at all three places. Here, in the avenue at the cemetery, he's looking at me curiously, as if wondering why I was photographing the crowd and not the coffin or the family.'

'It's true. He doesn't look worried, or preoccupied. Leave these photographs with me. I'm going to look at them in my own time. Thanks, Van Hamme. Tell Moers I'm very happy with the work you've done.'

'In that case,' Lapointe asked once he was on his own with Maigret, 'shall I go to the Ile Saint-Louis and show people the photograph of the girl?'

'It'll probably turn out to be pointless, but it's worth a try. Check if Janvier is back.'

Janvier quickly stepped into the office and glanced curiously at the pile of photographs.

'There you are, Janvier. I'd like you to go to the Sorbonne. I think it'll be easy for you to go to the office and find out what courses Antoine Batille attended most assiduously.'

'So I'm to question his fellow students?'

'Exactly. He may not have had any real friends, but he must sometimes have chatted to other students.

'Here, first of all, is a photograph showing a girl who seemed to be upset at the funeral this morning, and who followed the coffin all the way to the cemetery. Someone might have met him with her. Maybe they've just heard of her.'

'I get it.'

'This one shows a man in a raincoat who was at Quai d'Anjou, then opposite the church and finally at Montparnasse Cemetery. Show them that one too, just in case. I hope there's a class this afternoon and you'll be able to wait for them coming out.'

'You don't want me to question the professor?'

'I don't think they get to know their students. But hang on! Here's another photograph. It may have nothing to do with the case, but we mustn't neglect anything.'

A quarter of an hour later, Maigret was brought the newspaper cutting with the word 'No!' added in green ink. The word had been written in block letters almost two centimetres high, and underlined with a firm stroke. The exclamation mark was a good centimetre longer.

It looked like a vehement protest. Whoever had written those characters must have been indignant at the idea that a pathetic character like the former sailor could have been taken for the Rue Popincourt murderer.

Maigret sat motionless over the newspaper cutting and the photographs for more than a quarter of an hour, drawing gently on his pipe, after which, almost automatically, he picked up the phone.

'Hello . . . Frémiet? . . . I was worried you might have left. Thanks for the document, which seems really interesting. At first I thought of putting a small advertisement in tomorrow's morning paper, but it's possible that he doesn't read classifieds.

'There's bound to be another article on the case.'

'Our reporters are studying previous burglaries. I have a number of them working within a radius of fifty kilometres of Paris, showing the photographs of the gangsters to all the neighbours in the villas they've visited.'

'Could you publish the following lines below the article or articles:

' "Detective Chief Inspector Maigret would like to know what the sender of this message to the newspaper bases his claim upon. He asks him, if he has interesting information, to be so kind as to contact him either by letter or by telephone." '

'I understand. Could you repeat it, so that I'm sure of every word?'

Maigret repeated patiently.

'Fine! Not only will I publish this announcement on the first page, I'll put it in a frame. You must realize that you're going to be receiving letters or phone calls from lunatics.'

Maigret smiled.

'I'm used to it. You are too. The police and newspaper offices.'

'Right. You'll be so good as to keep me informed.'

And the inspector immersed himself in the evening newspapers which had just been brought to him, groaning every time he found a new inaccuracy. There was an average of one, or at the very least an exaggeration, per paragraph, and the art thieves were becoming one of the most mysterious and best organized in Paris.

Last headline:

When will the mastermind be arrested?

It was like the television news!

He had sent the article and the photograph of the sailor with the 'No!' in green letters to the anthropometry department for any fingerprints that they might be able to take from it. The reply came quickly.

'A thumb on the photograph, and a very good image of the index finger on the back of the paper. They don't correspond to any prints on file.'

That meant, obviously, that Antoine Batille's murderer had never been arrested and, more to the point, that he had never been convicted.

Maigret wasn't surprised, and he was about to resume reading his papers, when Lapointe came rushing in, very excited.

'A lucky break, chief. And you were right. Crossing the footbridge, I notice that I've run out of cigarettes. I go to Rue Saint-Louis-en-l'Ile. I go into the café on the corner, and who do I see?'

'The girl whose photograph I gave you.'

'Exactly. She's a waitress. Black dress and white apron. There was a table of people playing cards: the butcher, the grocer, the landlord and a man with his back to me. I got my cigarettes and went and sat down.

'When she asked me what I wanted to drink, I ordered

a coffee, and she went behind the counter to make me an espresso.

'"What time do you close in the evening?"'

'She looked at me with surprise.

'"It depends on the evening. I finish at seven, because I open up in the morning."'

'She gave me my change and went off without paying me any more attention. I preferred not to talk to her in front of the landlord. I said to myself that you'd rather do it yourself.'

'You're right.'

'She seems constantly about to burst into tears. She comes and goes as if she's in a daze and her nose is red.'

Janvier didn't get back to headquarters until six o'clock.

'There was a Sociology class, and apparently he never missed that one. I waited in the courtyard. I saw the students at their desks and, once the class was finished, they hurried into the open air.

'I questioned one, two, three, without success.

'"Antoine Batille? . . . The one who's in the papers? . . . I see, yes, but we didn't spend time together. If you could find a person called Harteau."'

The third student to be questioned had looked around, and suddenly called out, turning towards a young man who was walking away:

'Harteau! Harteau! It's for you.'

And, to Janvier:

'I've got to go. I have a train to catch.'

Others were leaving on motorbikes and scooters.

'You want to talk to me?' asked a tall young man with a pale face and light-grey eyes.

'I gather you were Antoine Batille's friend.'

'Friend is too strong a word. He didn't make friends easily. Let's say that I was a classmate, and we occasionally chatted in the courtyard and sometimes went for a drink together. I only went to his place once and I didn't feel comfortable. I should say that I'm the son of a concierge on Place Denfert-Rochereau. I'm not ashamed of it. At his place I didn't know where to put myself.'

'Were you at the funeral this morning?'

'Only at the church. After that I had an important class.'

'Do you know if your classmate had any enemies?'

'I'm sure he didn't.'

'Was he popular?'

'He wasn't popular either. Nobody paid him any attention, and he minded his own business too.'

'What about you? What did you think of him?'

'He was a decent guy. He was a lot more sensitive than he wanted to let on. I think he was too sensitive and he tended to close himself away.'

'Did he talk to you about his tape recorder?'

'I think he even asked me to come with him one day. He was wild about it. He claimed that people's voices were more revealing than their picture as it appeared in photographs. I remember one thing he said:

' "There are lots of picture-hunters. I'm not yet aware of any sound-hunters."

'He hoped to be given one of those miniature tape recorders made in Japan for Christmas. The ones you can hold in the palm of your hand. They don't yet have them in France, but apparently they're waiting for them. He would only have known them from magazine articles.'

Janvier hadn't neglected to ask Harteau if Batille had any girlfriends.

'No girlfriends, no. At any rate not that I knew of. It wasn't his style. And he was shy and reserved. But he'd been in love for a few weeks . . .

'He couldn't help talking to me about it. He had to confide in somebody, and his sister used to make fun of him, claiming that he was the girl and she was the boy of the house.

'I didn't see the girl, but she works on Ile Saint-Louis, and he saw her at eight o'clock every morning. That was the time when she was alone in the café. The landlord was still asleep, and the landlady was doing the housework on the first floor.

'They were constantly interrupted by customers, but they did still manage to have some time to themselves.'

'Was it really serious?'

'I think so.'

'What were his intentions?'

'From what point of view?'

'How did he see his future, for example?'

'He planned to take classes in Anthropology next year. His dream was to be appointed professor in Asia, in Africa, in South America, one after the other, so that he could study the different human races. He wanted to prove that they were all essentially the same, that differences would vanish as living conditions balanced out on all latitudes.'

'Did he plan to marry?'

'He wasn't yet talking about that. It's too recent. In any case, he didn't want to marry a girl from the same social class as himself.'

'Was he rebelling against his parents, against his family?'

'It wasn't even that. I remember he said to me one day: "When I go back home I feel as if I'm in 1900."'

'Thank you. Sorry for taking up your time.'

And Janvier concluded:

'What do you say, chief? What if that girl has a brother? What if they went further than young Harteau thinks? What if the brother got it into his head that the son of Mylène Perfumes would never marry his sister? You see what I'm getting at . . .'

'You're starting to sound a bit nineteenth-century, Janvier, old man.'

'These things still happen, don't they?'

'Haven't you read the statistics? So-called crimes of passion have declined by over half and will soon seem like a quaint anachronism.

'In fact Lapointe has found her, and she does work on Ile Saint-Louis. I'll try and have a chat with her tonight.'

'What should I do now?'

'Nothing. Anything. Everyday tasks. We'll wait.'

At 6.15, Maigret was having an early-evening drink at the Brasserie Dauphine, where he met up with two of his colleagues. At the office they sometimes spent whole weeks without seeing each other, each one confined in his own department. The Brasserie Dauphine was the neutral terrain where everyone finally met up.

'So, that murder in Rue Popincourt? Are you starting to work for Rue des Saussaies now?'

At 6.50 Maigret took a stroll along Rue Saint-Louis-en-l'Ile and could see the girl in the café, serving the customers.

The landlady was at the till, the landlord was serving at the bar. It was the brief flurry of early-evening aperitifs.

At 7.05 the girl went through a door and came back out a few moments later in the coat that she was wearing in the photograph. She said a few words to the landlady and left. She made straight for Quai d'Anjou, without looking around, and Maigret had to quicken his pace to catch up with her.

'Excuse me, mademois—'

She misunderstood and started to run.

'I'm Detective Chief Inspector Maigret. I'd like to talk to you about Antoine.'

She stopped dead and looked at him with an anxious expression.

'What did you say?'

'That I wanted to talk to you about . . .'

'I heard you. But I don't understand. I don't . . .'

'There's no point denying it.'

'Who told you?'

'Your photograph, or rather your photographs. You were outside the dead boy's house this morning, with a handkerchief clenched in your fingers. You were there when the funeral service started and when it ended and then you were at the cemetery.'

'Why was my photograph taken?'

'If you would take a moment and walk with me, I'll explain. We're looking for Antoine Batille's murderer. We don't have any serious trails, no useful clues.

'In the hope that this murderer would be attracted by the funeral of his victim, I had photographs taken of the rows of onlookers. Then the photographer looked to see who could be found at Quai d'Anjou, outside the church and at the cemetery.'

She bit her lips. They walked quite naturally along the embankment and passed in front of the building where the Batilles lived. The black drapes with their silver tassels had disappeared. The windows were lit on every floor. The house had resumed its usual rhythm of life.

'What do you want from me?'

'I want you to tell me everything you know about Antoine. You were the person closest to him.'

She blushed suddenly.

'What makes you say that?'

'He said it, in a different way. He had a classmate at the Sorbonne.'

'The concierge's son?'

'Yes.'

'He was the only one. He didn't feel at ease with the others. He always had a sense of being different.'

'Well, he gave this fellow Harteau to understand that one day he was going marry you.'

'Are you sure he said that?'

'Didn't he say it to you?'

'No. I wouldn't have accepted. We were from different worlds.'

'Perhaps he wasn't from any world except his own.'

'Besides, his parents . . .'

'How long had you known him?'

'Since I've been working at the café. That's four months. It was in the winter, I remember. It snowed the first day I saw him. He was buying a pack of Gitanes. He came in to get a pack every day.'

'How long was it before he waited for you when you were leaving work?'

'Over a month.'

'Did you become his girlfriend?'

'Just a week ago today.'

'Do you have a brother?'

'I've got two. One in the army, in Germany, the other works in Lyon.'

'Are you from Lyon?'

'My father was from Lyon. Now that he's dead, the family has dispersed, and I'm alone in Paris with my mother. We live on Rue Saint-Paul. I worked in a big store, but I couldn't cope. It was too tiring for me. When I found out that they were looking for a waitress in Rue Saint-Louis-en-l'Ile . . .'

'Did Antoine have any enemies?'

'Why would he have had enemies?'

'Because he liked taking his tape recorder round some very seedy places.'

'Nobody paid him any attention. He sat in a corner or leaned on the bar. He took me with him twice.'

'Did you meet up every evening?'

'He came to get me from the bar and brought me home. Once or twice a week we went to the cinema.'

'Can you tell me what your name is?'

'Mauricette.'

'Mauricette what?'

'Mauricette Gallois.'

They had slowly turned back, crossed Pont Marie and were now in Rue Saint-Paul.

'This is my place. Is there anything more you want to ask me?'

'Not for now. Thank you, Mauricette. Good luck.'

Maigret sighed and, by Saint-Paul Métro station, he took a taxi that brought him home in a few minutes. He tried not to think about his investigation and, after turning on the television out of habit, he turned it off again for fear that it might be talking about Rue Popincourt and the art thieves again.

'What are you thinking about?'

'That we could go to the cinema and that it's almost mild this evening. We'll be able to walk all the way to the Grands Boulevards.'

It was one of his favourite pastimes. After a few steps, Madame Maigret took his arm, and they walked along slowly, stopping from time to time to look at a window display. They talked about nothing in particular, a passing face, a dress, the last letter from his sister-in-law.

That evening, Maigret fancied a western, and they had to go all the way to Porte Saint-Denis to find one. In the interval he had a glass of calvados, and his wife settled for a verbena tea.

At midnight, the lights went out in their apartment. It hadn't occurred to Maigret that the previous day had been the first day of spring. It had turned up right on time. He saw again the light on Quai d'Anjou in the morning, outside the dead boy's house.

At nine o'clock he had a phone call from Poiret, the examining magistrate.

'Any news, Maigret?'

'Nothing so far. At any rate, nothing precise.'

'You don't think that sailor . . . What's his name again? . . . Yvon Demarle . . .'

'I'm convinced that while he's up to his neck in the art theft case, he has nothing to do with the murder in Rue Popincourt.'

'Do you have an idea?'

'It may be taking shape. It's still too vague to talk about, but I expect certain developments quite soon.'

'A crime of passion?'

'I don't think so.'

'Financially motivated?'

He hated these classifications.

'I don't know yet.'

He wouldn't have to wait long to find out. The phone rang half an hour later. It was the desk editor at one of the evening papers.

'Inspector Maigret? . . . This is Jean Rolland . . . I'm not disturbing you? . . . Don't worry. I'm not calling you for information, although if you have any it would always be welcome . . .'

Maigret was rather chilly with the editor of that

newspaper, precisely because he complained about not always being told important news items before anybody else.

'We print as much as three other newspapers . . . It would be natural . . .'

It wasn't war between them, more a sort of sulk. That was probably why the desk editor called him rather than his boss.

'Did you read our articles yesterday?'

'I've skimmed them.'

'We've tried to analyse the possibility of a close relationship between the two cases. In the end, we've found as many clues for as against.'

'I know.'

'And yet this article brought us a letter which we found in the morning mail, that I'm going to read to you.'

'Just one moment. Is the address written in block letters?'

'Yes. The letter, too.'

'I imagine it's on ordinary paper of the kind that they sell in packs of six in tobacconists' and grocers'.'

'Right again. Have you had another letter?'

'No. Go on.'

'I'll read it:

Dear sir,

I have read with care the articles published over the last few days in your estimable newspaper about what is called the Rue Popincourt affair and the affair of the paintings. Your editor is attempting, unsuccessfully, to establish a connection between the two affairs.

I find it naive on the part of the press to imagine that young Batille was attacked on Rue Popincourt because of a tape. And in any case, did the murderer take his tape recorder away?

As to the sailor Demarle, he has never killed anyone with his Swedish knife.

Those knives are sold in every good ironmongery, and I have one myself.

Except that mine really did kill Antoine Batille. I'm not boasting, believe me. I'm not proud of it. On the contrary. But I'm weary of all this fuss. And most importantly I don't want an innocent man like Demarle to pay in my place.

You may publish this letter if you see fit. I guarantee that it is only the truth.

Thank you.

Yours faithfully.

Of course, there was no signature.

'Do you think it's a joke, inspector?'

'No.'

'Is it serious?'

'I'm sure it is. Obviously I could be wrong, but there is a strong likelihood that this letter was written by the murderer. Look at the envelope and tell me where it was posted.'

'Boulevard Saint-Michel.'

'You can take a photograph of it if you plan to publish

a facsimile, but I'd like it to pass through as few hands as possible.'

'Do you hope to find prints?'

'I'm nearly certain that we'll find them.'

'Were there any on the newspaper cutting on which someone wrote the word "No!" in green ink?'

'Yes.'

'I read your appeal. Do you hope that the murderer will call you?'

'If he's the kind of man I think he is, he will.'

'I suppose there's no point in asking you what kind of man he is.'

'For now, in fact, I'm obliged to keep quiet. I'll send you someone to pick up that letter and I'll give it back to you once the case is over.'

'Fine. Good luck.'

He turned back towards the door in surprise. Joseph, the old clerk, was standing in the doorway and, behind him, there was a man in a beige uniform with big brown stripes on his trousers. His cap was beige too, and had a badge with a gold crown.

'This gentleman is insisting on giving you a small package in person, and I haven't been able to get rid of him.'

'What is it?' Maigret asked the intruder.

'It's a message from Monsieur Lherbier.'

'The leather merchant?'

'Yes.'

'Are you expecting a reply?'

'I wasn't told, but I was asked to hand this package to

you in person. It was Monsieur Lherbier himself who gave me the task yesterday evening.'

Maigret had unwrapped a beige cardboard box, marked with the inevitable crown, and in the box he found a black crocodile-skin wallet, the four corners reinforced with gold. Here again the crown was in gold.

A visiting card read only:

A token of my gratitude.

Maigret put the wallet back in the box.

'Just one moment,' he said to the messenger. 'You'll probably be better than me at rewrapping this package.'

The man looked at him in surprise.

'You don't like it?'

'Tell your boss that I'm not in the habit of receiving gifts. Add if you wish that I am still touched by his gesture.'

'Aren't you going to write to him?'

'No.'

The telephone rang insistently.

'Right! Carry on rewrapping your package in the waiting room. I'm very busy.'

And once he was on his own again, he picked up the phone.

6.

'It's someone who doesn't want to give his name, inspector. Shall I put him through anyway? He claims you know who he is.'

'Put him through.'

He heard the click and said in a voice that wasn't entirely his usual one:

'Hello.'

Maigret and his interlocutor were equally impressed, and the inspector was careful to avoid anything that might startle the person on the other end.

'Do you know who's speaking?'

'Yes.'

'Do you know my name?'

'Your name isn't important.'

'Aren't you going to try and find out where I'm calling from?'

The voice was hesitant. The man lacked confidence and was trying to embolden himself.

'No.'

'Why?'

'Because I'm not interested.'

'Don't you believe me?'

'I do.'

'Do you believe that I'm the man from Rue Popincourt?'

'Yes.'

This time there was quite a long silence, then the voice asked shyly, anxiously:

'Are you still there?'

'Yes. I'm listening.'

'Have you already been given the letter that I sent to the newspaper?'

'No, it was read out to me on the phone.'

'Did you receive the cutting with the photograph?'

'Yes.'

'Do you believe me? You don't think I'm a lunatic?'

'I've already told you.'

'What do you think of me?'

'First of all, I know that you have no criminal record.'

'Because of my prints?'

'Exactly. You're used to leading a modest and regular life.'

'How can you tell?'

Maigret fell silent, and the other man began to panic again.

'Don't hang up.'

'Do you have lots of things to tell me?'

'I don't know . . . Perhaps . . . I have no one to talk to . . .'

'You aren't married, are you?'

'No.'

'You live alone. Today you've taken the day off, perhaps calling your office to tell them you were ill.'

'You're trying to make me say things that will help you

identify me. Are you sure that your technicians aren't trying to trace my call?'

'I give you my word.'

'So you're not in a hurry to arrest me?'

'I'm like you. I'm glad it's over.'

'How do you know?'

'You wrote to the papers.'

'I don't want them to go after an innocent man.'

'That's not the real reason.'

'Do you think I want to be caught?'

'Unconsciously, yes.'

'What else do you think about me?'

'You feel lost.'

'The truth is that I'm afraid.'

'Afraid of what? Of being arrested?'

'No. It doesn't matter. I've already said too much. I wanted to talk to you, to hear your voice. Do you despise me?'

'I don't despise anybody.'

'Not even a criminal?'

'Not even a criminal!'

'You know you'll catch me sooner or later, isn't that so?'

'Yes.'

'Do you have clues?'

Maigret nearly admitted to him, to get it over with, that he already had a photograph of him, first at Quai d'Anjou, then outside the church, and finally at Montparnasse Cemetery.

He would only have to publish these photographs in the papers for a number of people to give him the identity of Batille's murderer.

If he didn't, it was because he had a hunch that in that case the man wouldn't wait to be arrested, and that they would probably find a corpse at his home.

He had to come forward of his own accord, slowly.

'There are still clues, but it's hard to assess their value.'

'I'm about to hang up.'

'What are you going to do today?'

'What do you mean?'

'It's Saturday. Are you going to spend Sunday in the country?'

'Of course not.'

'Have you got a car?'

'No.'

'You work in an office, don't you?'

'That's true. There are tens of thousands of offices in Paris, I can tell you that.'

'Do you have friends?'

'No.'

'A girlfriend?'

'No. When I have to, I take what I can get . . . You know what I mean?'

'I'm sure that tomorrow you'll take advantage of the fact that it's Sunday to write a long letter to the papers.'

'How come you guess everything?'

'Because you aren't the first person this has happened to.'

'And how did it work out for the others?'

'There were different endings.'

'Did some of them kill themselves?'

He didn't reply, and there was silence at the end of the line again.

'I don't have a gun and I know that these days it's almost impossible to get hold of one without a special permit.'

'You're not going to commit suicide.'

'What makes you think that?'

'You wouldn't have called me.'

Maigret wiped his forehead. This conversation seemed almost banal. Yet these trivial exchanges were still allowing him to get the man's character in focus.

'I'm going to hang up,' said the voice at the end of the line.

'You can call me again on Monday.'

'Not tomorrow?'

'It's Sunday tomorrow, and I won't be in the office.'

'Won't you be at home?'

'I'm planning to go to the country with my wife.'

Each phrase was deliberate.

'You're lucky.'

'Yes.'

'Are you a happy man?'

'Relatively, like most men.'

'I've never been happy.'

He hung up abruptly. Either someone had tried to get into the booth, impatient at seeing him talking for such a long time, or the conversation had left his nerves raw.

He wasn't a drinker. Perhaps, to give himself courage, he would make an exception? He had called from a café or a bar. People were rubbing shoulders with him, looking at him without suspecting that he was a killer.

Maigret called his wife.

'What would you say to spending the weekend in Meung-sur-Loire?'

She was so startled that she said nothing for a moment.

'But . . . you . . . What about your investigation?'

'It needs to stew.'

'When would we leave?'

'After lunch.'

'By car?'

'Of course.'

Even though she had been driving for a year, she still wasn't confident, and she always took the wheel with uncontrollable apprehension.

'Buy something for dinner this evening, because the shops may be closed by the time we get there. And something to make a large breakfast with tomorrow morning. We'll have lunch at the inn.'

Among his closest colleagues the only one available was good old Janvier, and he invited him to go for a drink.

'What are you doing tomorrow?'

'You know, chief, Sunday is the day for my mother-in-law, the children's uncles and aunts.'

'We're going to Meung.'

He and his wife had lunch quickly at Boulevard Richard-Lenoir. Then, after doing the washing up, Madame Maigret went and changed.

'Is it cold?'

'Chilly.'

'Can I wear my floral dress?'

'Why not? You're taking a coat, aren't you?'

An hour later, they entered the flow of tens of thousands of Parisians heading for a patch of green.

They found the house as clean and tidy as if they had

left it the previous day, because a local woman came in twice a week to air it, dust it and clean the parquet floor. There was no point talking to her about new cleaning products. Everything was waxed, even the furniture, and there was a strong smell of polish.

Her husband looked after the garden, and Maigret found crocuses in the lawn and, at the foot of the back wall, in the most sheltered spot, daffodils and tulips.

His first concern was to go to the first floor to put on an old pair of trousers and a flannel shirt. He always felt that the house, with its exposed beams and dark corners, and the peace that reigned there, was like a priest's house. He wasn't unhappy with this, quite the contrary.

Madame Maigret busied herself in the kitchen.

'Are you very hungry?'

'Normally hungry.'

They didn't have a television down here. After dinner, when the weather was a little warmer, they sat in the garden and watched twilight fall and darken the landscape.

That evening they went for a gentle walk, going down to the Loire, which, after the rains earlier that week, rolled with muddy water and swept tree branches along.

'Are you worried?'

He had been silent for a long time.

'Not exactly. Antoine Batille's killer called me this morning.'

'To taunt you? Out of defiance?'

'No. He needed reassurance.'

'And he turned to you?'

'There was no one else available to him.'

'Are you sure he was the murderer?'

'I said the killer. A murder assumes premeditation.'

'His act wasn't premeditated?'

'Not exactly, unless I'm mistaken.'

'Why did he write to the papers?'

'Did you read that?'

'Yes. At first, I thought it was a prank. Do you know who he is?'

'No, but I could find out in twenty-four hours.'

'Aren't you interested in arresting him?'

'He'll give himself up of his own accord.'

'And what if he doesn't give himself up? If he commits another crime.'

'I don't think that . . .'

But Maigret was in a state of suspense. Was he right to be so sure of himself? He thought of Antoine Batille, who had dreamed of studying tropical people and who wanted to marry young Mauricette.

He wasn't yet twenty-one, and he had been brought down in a deluge in Rue Popincourt, never to get back to his feet.

He slept badly. Twice he opened his eyes, thinking that he heard the phone ringing.

'He won't kill again.'

He tried to reassure himself.

'Basically he's the one who's frightened.'

A real Sunday sun, a sun of childhood memories. Beneath the dew, the garden smelled good, and the house smelled of eggs and ham.

The day passed uneventfully; still, Maigret's face

seemed to be behind a veil. He couldn't relax completely, and his wife was aware of it.

At the inn they were welcomed with open arms and they had to clink glasses with everyone, because they were almost considered as locals.

'A game of cards this afternoon?'

Why not? They ate local rillettes made locally, *coq au vin blanc* and, after goat's cheese, rum babas.

'About four o'clock?'

'Of course.'

He looked for the most sheltered corner of the garden to set down his wicker armchair and, with the sun warming his eyelids, he soon fell asleep.

When he woke up, Madame Maigret made him a cup of coffee.

'It was a pleasure to see you sleeping so well.'

He had something like a taste of the countryside in his mouth, and he thought he could still hear the flies buzzing around him.

'Wasn't it strange to hear his voice on the telephone?'

Neither of them could help thinking about it, each in their own way.

'After forty years in the job, I'm still impressed when I encounter a man who has killed.'

'Why?'

'Because he has crossed the line.'

He didn't provide any further information. He knew what he meant. A man who kills cuts himself off in a sense from the human community. In the blink of an eye, he stops being an individual like the rest.

He wanted to explain himself, to say that. He had the words on the tip of his tongue but he knew that it was no use, no one would understand him.

Even real killers, professionals. Their manner is aggressive, sarcastic; it's because they need to show off, to make themselves believe that they still exist as men.

'Will you be getting back very late?'

'I hope to be back before six thirty.'

He met up with his old friends from the town, sound people for whom he wasn't the famous Detective Chief Inspector Maigret but a neighbour and also an excellent fisherman. The red mat was spread out in front of them. The cards, which had seen better days, were slightly sticky. The local white wine was cool and fresh.

'Your call.'

'Diamonds.'

His opponent on the left announced a sequence of three, his partner four queens.

'Trumps.'

The afternoon was spent playing cards, fanning them out, announcing runs of three or royal pairs. It was like a restful hum. From time to time the landlord came in to take a look at how each of them was playing and left again with a knowing smile.

Sunday must have seemed like a long day to the man who had killed Antoine Batille. Maigret hoped that he hadn't stayed at home. Did he have a small apartment, with his own furniture, or did he pay for a room by the month, in a modest hotel?

It was better for him not to stay within four walls, to

go outside and lose himself in the crowd, or perhaps go to the cinema.

In Rue Popincourt, on Tuesday evening, it was raining so hard that it looked like a cataclysm, and fishing boats had been lost in the Channel and the North Sea.

Wasn't that important in its way? And perhaps also in its way Antoine's jacket, his long hair?

Maigret tried not to think about it, to concentrate on the game.

'So, inspector, what do you say?'

'I'll pass.'

The white wine had gone to his head a little. He wasn't used to it any more. It went down like cool water, and it was only later that you felt the effects.

'I'll have to be getting back.'

'We'll stop at five hundred points, all right?'

'Let's go for five hundred points.'

He lost and paid for the rounds.

'It looks as if you've been neglecting your game in Paris. A bit rusty, aren't you?'

'A bit, yes.'

'You'll have to come for a bit longer at Easter.'

'I hope so. It's the best I can hope for. There are criminals who . . .'

And there it was! All of a sudden, he was thinking about the phone call again.

'Good evening, gentlemen.'

'See you next Saturday?'

'Maybe.'

He wasn't disappointed. He had had the weekend he

had decided to have, but he couldn't hope that his worries and responsibilities wouldn't follow him to the country.

'At what time do you want to leave?'

'As soon as we've had something to eat. What have you got for dinner?'

'Old Bambois came and gave me a tench, and I cooked it in the oven.'

He went and looked greedily at the swollen skin, a beautiful golden colour.

They drove slowly, because Madame Maigret was even more anxious by night than by day. Maigret turned on the radio and smiled as he listened to the traffic warnings, then the day's news.

It was mostly about foreign politics, and Maigret sighed with relief as he noted that there was nothing about the affair in Rue Popincourt.

In other words, the murderer had behaved himself. No crime. No suicide. Only the kidnapping of a little girl in Bouches-du-Rhône. They still hoped to find her alive.

He slept better than the night before, and it was broad daylight when he was woken by a lorry whose exhaust pipe sounded as if it was exploding. His wife was no longer beside him.

She had probably just got up, because the bed was still warm, and she was busy making coffee in the kitchen.

Leaning on the banisters, Madame Maigret watched her husband going heavily downstairs, a little as if she was watching a child going off to sit a difficult exam. She knew barely any more than the newspapers, but what the newspapers didn't know was how much energy he put into trying to understand, how much he concentrated during certain investigations. It was as if he identified with the people he was hunting and suffered the same torments as they did.

He was lucky enough to find an open-platform bus, and that way he was able to go on smoking his first pipe of the morning.

No sooner had he arrived in his office than Detective Chief Inspector Grosjean called him on the phone.

'How's it going, Maigret?'

'Very well. And you? Those shady characters?'

'Contrary to what one might have believed, it was Gouvion, the pathetic lookout, who was most useful to us, and who allowed us to find witnesses for two of the burglaries, at the Château de l'Épine, near Arpajon, and the other in a villa in Dreux Forest.

'Gouvion often spent three or four days on the spot, watching comings and goings. Sometimes he went for lunch or a drink nearby.

'I think he'll crack soon and spill the beans. His wife, who used to be an actress at Châtelet, is begging him to do it.

'All four of them are at the Santé, in different cells.

'I wanted to keep you up to date and say thank you again.

'What about your case?'

'It's going very slowly.'

Half an hour later, as he expected, it was the editor of the morning newspaper wanting to speak to him.

'Another message?'

'Yes. Except that this one didn't come by post, but was put in our letterbox.'

'Is it long?'

'Quite long. The envelope says: "To be given to the author of Saturday's article about the crime in Rue Popincourt."'

'In block letters again?'

'He seems to write very fluently like that. Shall I read it to you?'

'If you would be so kind.'

Dear sir,

I have read your most recent articles, in particular the one on Saturday, and while I cannot judge their literary value, I have a sense that you are really seeking the truth. The same cannot be said of some of your colleagues, who seek sensations, print anything at all and then contradict themselves the next day

But I have one reproach to make to you. In the course of your last article you speak of the 'lunatic' in Rue Popincourt. Why that word, which is insulting first of all, and which also implies a judgement? Because there were seven knife blows? Probably, because you say later on that the murderer struck like a madman.

Do you know that with words of this kind you can do a lot of harm? Some situations are painful enough in themselves without being judged superficially.

It reminds me of that minister of the interior, not so long ago, talking about a fifteen-year-old boy and using the word 'monster', which of course the whole of the press picked up.

I don't ask to be treated with kid gloves. I know that people only see me as a killer. But I would like not to be troubled in addition by words that probably exceed the thoughts of those who use them.

Otherwise, thank you for your objectivity.

I can tell you that I have telephoned Detective Chief Inspector Maigret. He seemed understanding, and one is inclined to confide in him. But to what extent does his job not oblige him to play a part, if not to set traps?

I think I will phone him again. I feel very tired. Tomorrow, however, I'm going to go back to work at the office. I'm an ordinary paper pusher.

On Saturday I attended Antoine Batille's funeral. I saw his father, his mother and his sister. I would like them to know that I had no complaints about their son. I didn't know him. I had never seen him. I am sincerely repentant about the harm I have done them.

Yours sincerely.

'Shall I publish it?'

'I don't see any reason not to. On the contrary. It will encourage him to write again, and in each letter we learn a bit more. When you've been able to photocopy the letter, please be so kind as to send it to me. You don't need to have it brought by messenger.'

The phone call didn't come until 12.30, when Maigret wondered whether he should go for lunch.

'I suppose you're calling me from a café or a bar near your office?'

'That's right. Are you in a hurry?'

'I was about to leave for lunch.'

'Didn't you know that I was going to call you?'

'I did.'

'Have you read my letter? I suspected that they would phone you. That's why I didn't send you a copy.'

'You need the public to read your words, don't you?'

'I'd like them not to get the wrong idea. Because a person has killed, people get the wrong idea about him. You do too, probably.'

'You know, I've seen a lot of them.'

'I know.'

'In the days of forced labour, some people used to write to me from Guyana. Others, once their sentence is over, sometimes come and see me.'

'Really?'

'Do you feel a bit better?'

'I don't know. In any case, this morning, I was able to work more or less normally. It's strange to think that these same people who treat me quite naturally would become completely different if I just uttered one little phrase.'

'Do you want to utter it?'

'There are times when I have to restrain myself. With my office manager, for example, who looks down on me.'

'Were you born in Paris?'

'No. In a small provincial town, I won't tell you which one, because it would help you to identify me.'

'What did your father do?'

'He's head accountant in a . . . let's say quite an important company. Their right-hand man, you understand.
The idiot that the bosses can keep there until ten o'clock
at night and make him come in on Saturday afternoon if
not Sunday.'

'And your mother?'

'She's in poor health. As far back as I go in my memories,
I always see her ill. Apparently it started after I was born.'

'Do you have any brothers or sisters?'

'No. For that very reason. She still keeps the house,
which is very clean. When I went to school, I was one of
the best turned out among the pupils too.

'My parents are proud people. They would have liked
me to become a lawyer, or a doctor. I'd had enough of
studying. Then they thought I would go into the company
that my father works for, which is the biggest company
in the town. I didn't want to stay there. I felt I was suffocating. I came to Paris.'

'Where you're suffocating in an office, aren't you?'

'Except that as soon as I leave no one knows me. I'm
free.'

He was talking more easily, more naturally than the last
time. He was less frightened. There were fewer silences.

'What do you think of me?'

'Didn't you ask me that already?'

'I'm talking about me in general. Disregarding Rue
Popincourt.'

'I think there are tens, hundreds of thousands of people
in a similar situation.'

'Most of them are married and have children.'

'Why aren't you married? Because of your condition?'

'Do you really mean what you're saying?'

'Yes.'

'Every word?'

'Yes.'

'I don't understand you. You aren't how I imagined a detective chief inspector with the Police Judiciaire would be.'

'It's the same with everybody. Even at Quai des Orfèvres, we're all different from each other.'

'What I really don't understand is what you told me last time. You claimed you'd be able to identify me within twenty-four hours.'

'It's true.'

'How?'

'I'll tell you when we're face to face.'

'What reason do you have not to get on with it and arrest me straight away?'

'And what if I asked you what your reason was for killing?'

There was a silence even more troubling than the others, and Maigret wondered if he had gone too far.

'Hello,' he said.

'Yes.'

'I'm sorry for being harsh. You must face the facts.'

'I know. That's what I'm trying to do, believe me. Perhaps you imagine that I write for the papers and I'm calling you because I need to talk about me. Basically it's because it's all so wrong!'

'What's wrong?'

'What people think. The questions I'll be asked by the court if I'm ever brought to trial. The summing-up by the assistant public prosecutor. And even, perhaps especially, the plea by my lawyer.'

'Are you already thinking that far ahead?'

'You have to.'

'Are you planning on handing yourself in?'

'You think I'll be doing that soon, don't you?'

'Yes.'

'Do you think I'll be relieved?'

'I'm sure of it.'

'I'll be locked up in a cell and treated like . . .'

He didn't finish his sentence, and Maigret avoided intervening.

'I don't want to keep you longer. Your wife will be waiting for you.'

'I'm sure she won't be getting impatient. She's used to it.'

Silence again. It was as if he couldn't bring himself to break the line that connected him to another man.

'Are you happy?' he asked shyly, as if obsessed by the question.

'Relatively happy. That is to say, as happy as a man can be.'

'I've never been happy since the age of fourteen, not for a day, an hour, a minute.'

He abruptly changed his tone.

'Thank you.'

And he hung up.

In the afternoon Maigret had to go up to Poiret's office.

'How is your investigation coming along?' he asked with the hint of impatience common to all examining magistrates.

'It's practically over.'

'Does that mean you know the murderer?'

'He called me again this morning.'

'Who is it?'

Maigret took from his pocket the enlarged photograph of a face taken in the crowd, in the sun on Quai d'Anjou.

'Is it this young man?'

'He's not all that young. He's about thirty.'

'Have you arrested him?'

'Not yet.'

'Where does he live?'

'I don't know his name or his address. If I published this photograph, people who see him every day, his colleagues, his concierge – whoever – would recognize him and immediately tell me.'

'Why don't you?'

'That's the question that's troubling him too, and which he asked me for the second time this morning.'

'Had he called you already?'

'On Saturday, yes.'

'You realize, inspector, the responsibility that you're assuming. And in any case it's a responsibility that I share indirectly now that I've seen this photograph. I don't like that.'

'Neither do I. Except if I went too quickly, he probably wouldn't allow himself to be arrested, and would prefer to end it all.'

'Are you afraid that he'll kill himself?'

'He hasn't much to lose, don't you think?'

'Hundreds of criminals have been apprehended, and very few have taken their own lives.'

'What if he was of that type?'

'Has he written to the papers yet?'

'A letter was deposited in a newspaper's letterbox, yesterday evening or last night.'

'I think that mania is well known. If I remember my criminology courses correctly, it's usually the preserve of the paranoid.'

'According to psychiatrists, yes.'

'You don't agree with them?'

'I don't know enough to contradict them. The only difference between them and me is that I don't divide people into categories.'

'But it's necessary.'

'Necessary why?'

'To judge them, for example.'

'It's not my role to judge.'

'I was told that you'd be hard to handle.'

The magistrate said that with a faint smile, but he still meant it.

'Shall we do a deal? It's Monday. Let's say Wednesday at the same time . . .'

'I'm listening.'

'If your man isn't behind bars, you'll send his photograph to the papers.'

'You really want me to do that?'

'I'm giving you as much time as I think is necessary.'

'Thank you.'

Maigret went back down to his floor and opened the door to the inspectors' office. He didn't need them especially.

'Are you coming, Janvier?'

In his office he went over to the window and opened it, because he was hot, and the noise from outside suddenly filled the room. He sat down at his desk and chose a pipe with a curved stem that he smoked less often than the others.

'No news?'

'No news, chief.'

'Sit down.'

The magistrate hadn't understood. For him, criminals were defined by one article or another of the Penal Code.

Maigret also sometimes needed to think out loud.

'He called me again.'

'Has he decided to hand himself in?'

'He wants to. He's still hesitating, the way one hesitates to jump into icy water.'

'I suppose he trusts you?'

'I think so. But he knows it's not down to me. I'm just back from upstairs. When the examining magistrate starts questioning him, unfortunately he'll grasp certain realities.

'I know a bit more about him. He comes from a small provincial town, and preferred not to tell me which one. That means it's a very small town, where we would easily have been able to pick up his trail. His father is a head accountant, a right-hand man, as he says, not without bitterness.'

'I know the type.'

'They wanted him to be a lawyer or a doctor. He couldn't complete his studies. And he didn't want to go into the same company as his father either. That's not uncommon, as I told him.

'He's an office clerk. He lives alone. He has a reason for not getting married.'

'Did he tell you what?'

'No, but I think I understand.'

But Maigret avoided saying anything more on the subject.

'There's nothing I can do but wait. He will probably remind me tomorrow. On Wednesday afternoon, I will have to send his photograph to the newspapers.'

'Why?'

'An ultimatum from the examining magistrate. He doesn't want to assume the responsibility of waiting for longer than that.'

'Do you hope that—?'

The phone rang.

'It's your anonymous caller, inspector.'

'Hello . . . Monsieur Maigret? . . . Forgive me for hanging up on you this morning. There are moments when I say to myself that nothing makes any sense. I'm like a fly bumping into a window as it tries to escape the four walls of the room . . .'

'You're not in the office?'

'I went in. I did so in good faith. They gave me an urgent file. When I opened it and read the first few lines, I asked myself what I was doing there . . .

'I was seized by a sort of panic, and on the pretext of going to the toilet I went out into the corridor . . . I paused just long enough to grab my raincoat and hat in passing . . . I was worried that I was going to be caught, as if I felt I was being hunted down.'

At the start of the call, Maigret had gestured to Janvier to pick up the second receiver.

'What part of town are you in?'

'On the Grands Boulevards . . . I've been walking in the crowd for over an hour . . . There are times when I'm angry with you, when I suspect you of doing it on purpose to drive me mad, to put me gradually in such a state of mind that I will have no option left but to hand myself in . . .'

'Have you been drinking?'

'How can you tell?'

His voice grew more vehement.

'I've had two or three brandies.'

'Are you not in the habit of drinking?'

'Just a glass of wine with meals, the occasional aperitif.'

'Do you smoke?'

'No.'

'What are you going to do now?'

'I don't know . . . Nothing . . . Walk . . . Perhaps go and sit in a café to read the afternoon papers . . .'

'Have you sent any other messages?'

'No. I might write one, but I haven't got much left to say.'

'Do you live in a furnished apartment?'

'I own my own furniture and have access to a kitchenette and a bathroom.'

'Do you prepare your own meals?'

'I used to prepare my evening meal.'

'And you haven't done that for a few days?'

'That's right. I go home as late as possible . . . Why are you asking me such banal questions?'

'Because they help me to understand you.'

'Do you do the same thing with all your clients?'

'It varies from case to case.'

'Are they so different from each other?'

'All men are different . . . Why don't you come and see me?'

He giggled nervously.

'Would you let me go again?'

'I can't promise to do that.'

'You see? When I go and see you, as you say, that's when I will have made a definite decision.'

Maigret nearly talked to him about the examining magistrate's ultimatum, then he weighed the pros and cons and decided to keep quiet.

'Goodbye, inspector.'

'Goodbye. Good luck.'

Maigret and Janvier looked at one another.

'Poor guy!' Janvier murmured.

'He's still struggling with himself. He's lucid. He's not deluding himself. I wonder if he'll come before Wednesday.'

'Don't you have a sense that he's already hesitating?'

'He's been hesitating since Saturday. For now he's

outside, in the sunlight, in the crowd where no one is pointing at him. He can go into a café and order a brandy and they'll serve him without paying him any attention. He can go for dinner in a restaurant or sit in the darkness of a cinema.'

'I understand.'

'I'm putting myself in his place. At any moment . . .'

'If he committed suicide, as you fear, it would be even more final.'

'I know. But he's the one who should know that. I only hope he won't go on drinking . . .'

A draught of fresh air passed through the room, and Maigret looked at the open window.

'In fact, why don't we go for a drink?'

And, a few minutes later, they were both standing at the bar of the Brasserie Dauphine.

'A cognac,' Maigret ordered, while Janvier smiled.

7.

Tuesday was difficult. But Maigret was in very good spirits when he reached his office. It was such a fine spring day that he had walked the whole way from Boulevard Richard-Lenoir, sniffing the air, the smell of the shops, sometimes turning to look at the bright, cheerful dresses of the women.

'Nothing for me?'

It was nine o'clock.

'Nothing, chief.'

In a few minutes, in half an hour, one of the editors or editors-in-chief would call him to announce a new letter written in block letters.

He was counting on a decisive day. He had prepared for it and arranged his pipes on his desk, carefully chose one and went and lit it by the window while looking at the Seine sparkling in the morning sun.

When he had to attend the morning briefing, he had Janvier go and sit in his office.

'If he phones, make him wait and come and get me straight away.'

'Yes, chief.'

There was no phone call while he was in the commissioner's office. There wasn't one at ten o'clock. There still hadn't been one by eleven.

Maigret went through some mail, absent-mindedly filled in forms and, sometimes, as if to cheat time, went and spent a few minutes in the inspectors' office, taking care to leave his door open. Everyone felt worried, nervous.

This telephone that wasn't ringing created a sort of void that made him uneasy. Something was missing.

'Are you sure that there wasn't a call for me?'

He was the one who ended up phoning the papers.

'Have you had anything this morning?'

'Not this morning, no.'

The previous day, the first phone call from the man from Rue Popincourt had come in at 12.10. At midday, Maigret didn't go out with the others. He waited until half-past and, once again, asked Janvier, who knew most about the case, to take his place.

His wife didn't ask any questions; the answer was all too obvious.

Had he lost the game? Had he been wrong to trust his instinct? Tomorrow, at the same time, he would be obliged to go and see the examining magistrate and admit defeat. The photograph would be published in the papers.

What the hell could that idiot be doing? Rage surged through him in waves.

'He was only trying to make himself interesting, and now he's dropping me. Maybe he was making fun of how trusting I am.'

He went back to the office sooner than usual.

'Nothing?' he asked Janvier automatically.

Janvier would have given a lot to have good news to give him, because it was difficult to see his boss in this state.

'Not yet.'

The afternoon was even longer than the morning. Maigret tried in vain to take an interest in routine work, making the most of the opportunity to get through overdue paperwork. But his mind was elsewhere.

He imagined all the possible hypotheses and rejected them one by one. He even telephoned the police emergency number.

'Has anyone called you about suicides?'

'Just one moment . . . There was one during the night, an old woman who gassed herself, at Porte d'Orléans . . . A man threw himself into the Seine at eight o'clock this morning. We were able to save him.'

'What age?'

'Forty-two. Neurasthenic.'

Why was he so bothered? He had done what he could. It was time to face up to reality. He wasn't unhappy because he had been deceived, but because his intuition had failed him. Because then it was serious. It meant that he had lost touch and, in that case . . .

'Damn, damn and damn!'

He had said that at the top of his voice, in the solitude of his office, and he picked up his hat and went, without an overcoat, all alone, towards the Brasserie Dauphine, where he drank two large beers at the bar, one after the other.

'No phone call?' he asked as he came back.

By seven o'clock there had been no call, and he resigned himself to going home. He felt cumbersome, and not at peace with himself. He took a taxi. He didn't enjoy the sun, or the colourful bustle of the streets. He didn't even know what the weather was like.

He began heavily climbing the stairs and stopped twice because he was slightly out of breath. A few steps away from his landing he saw his wife, who was watching him come up.

She was waiting for him the way one waits for a child coming home from school, and he was about to get cross with her. When he was level with her, she merely said to him in an undertone:

'He's here.'

'Are you sure it's him?'

'He told me so himself.'

'Has he been here for a long time?'

'Nearly an hour.'

'Aren't you frightened?'

Maigret suddenly felt retrospectively afraid for his wife.

'I knew I wasn't in any danger.'

They whispered outside the door, which was ajar.

'We've been chatting.'

'About what?'

'About everything . . . spring . . . Paris . . . The little restaurants popular with taxi-drivers that are disappearing . . .'

Maigret came in at last and, in the living room which served as both a dining room and a drawing room, he saw a man, still young, rising to his feet. Madame Maigret had invited him to take off his raincoat, and he had set his hat down on a chair. He was wearing a navy-blue suit and looked younger than he was.

He forced a smile.

'Forgive me for coming here,' he said. 'Up at your office I was afraid that they wouldn't let me see you straight away. People tell so many stories.'

He must have been afraid of being beaten up. He was embarrassed and tried to find words to break the silence. He didn't realize that the inspector was as embarrassed as he was. Meanwhile, Madame Maigret had gone back into the kitchen.

'You're just as I imagined you would be.'

'Take a seat.'

'Your wife has been very patient with me.'

And, as if he had forgotten to do it until then, he took a Swedish knife from his pocket and held it out to Maigret.

'You'll be able to have the blood analysed. I haven't cleaned it.'

Maigret set it down casually on a pedestal table and sat down in an armchair facing his visitor.

'I don't know where to start . . . It's very difficult . . .'

'First of all I'm going to ask you some questions . . . What's your name?'

'Robert Bureau . . . Bureau like an office . . . You could say it's symbolic, because my father and I . . .'

'Where do you live?'

'I have a small lodging in Rue de l'École-de-Médecine, in a very old building at the end of the courtyard. I work in Rue Laffitte, for an insurance company. Or rather I did work. It's all over, isn't it?'

He uttered the phrase with melancholy resignation. He was serene and looked at his calm surroundings as if trying to become a part of them.

'What town do you come from originally?'

'Saint-Amand-Montrond, on the banks of the Cher. There's a big printworks there, the Mamin and Delvoye printworks, which does work for several Paris publishers. My father is a clerk there, and on his lips the names of Mamin and Delvoye are nearly sacred. We lived – my parents still do – in a small house near Canal de Berry . . .'

Maigret didn't want to rush him and get to the essential questions too quickly.

'You didn't like your town?'

'No.'

'Why not?'

'I felt as if I was suffocating there. Everyone knows everybody. When you walk down the street you see curtains twitching in the windows. I've always heard my parents murmuring:

' "What would people say?" '

'Were you a good student?'

'Until the age of fourteen and a half I was top of the class. My parents got so used to it that they told me off if I came down a mark in my report.'

'When did you begin to get frightened?'

Maigret had the impression that his interlocutor was becoming paler, that two little hollows formed near his nostrils, and that his lips were growing dry.

'I don't know how I've been able to keep the secret until now.'

'What happened when you were fourteen and a half?'

'Do you know the area?'

'I've passed through it.'

'The Cher runs parallel to the canal. In places it's only about ten metres away. It's broad and shallow, with stones and rocks that mean it can be forded.

'The banks are covered with reeds, willows and all kinds of shrubs. Especially towards Drevant, a village about three kilometres from Saint-Amand.

'That's where the local children go and play. I didn't play with them.'

'Why not?'

'My mother called them little hooligans. Some of them swam stark naked in the river. Almost all of them were the sons of print-workers, and my parents made a big distinction between the workers and the office clerks.

'There were about fifteen, maybe twenty of them playing. There were two girls with them. One of them, Renée, who must have been thirteen, was very shapely for her age and I was in love with her.

'I've thought of all that a lot, inspector, and I wonder if things might have happened differently. I suppose they might. I'm not trying to make excuses for myself.

'One boy, the butcher's son, kissed her in the bushes . . . I caught them . . . They went and swam with the others . . . The boy was called Raymond Pomel and he had red hair, like his father, from whom we bought our sausages . . .

'At one point he had gone off to relieve himself . . . He had come close to me without knowing and I took my knife out of my pocket and flicked out the blade . . .

'I swear I didn't know what I was doing . . . I stabbed him several times, with a sensation of freeing myself of something ... For me at that moment it was indispensable ... I wasn't committing a crime, killing a boy ... I stabbed ... I went on stabbing when he was on the ground, then I walked calmly away ...'

He had grown animated and his eyes were gleaming.

'They only discovered him two hours later ... They hadn't noticed that he was no longer with the gang of twenty or so kids ... I went home after washing the knife in the canal ...'

'How did you have that knife at such a young age?'

'I had stolen it a few months earlier from one of my uncles ... I was wild about penknives ... One Sunday at my uncle's I noticed that Swedish knife and took it ... My uncle looked for it everywhere without thinking of me for a moment ...'

'How did your mother not find it, for example?'

'The wall of our house, facing the garden, was covered with Virginia creeper and its dark foliage framed my window. When I didn't have my knife in my pocket, I hid it in the thickest part of the vine.'

'No one thought of you?'

'That's what surprised me. They arrested a sailor, whom they then had to release ... They thought of every possible suspect, except a child ...'

'What was your state of mind?'

'To tell you the truth, I felt no remorse. I listened to what the women said in the street, I read the newspaper from Montluçon which talked about the crime, without feeling concerned.

'I felt no emotion as I watched the funeral passing by ...

For me, at that moment, it was already part of the past . . . Part of the inevitable . . . I had nothing to do with it . . . I don't know if you understand? I think it's impossible, if you haven't been through it . . .

'I continued going to school, where I had become distracted, and my marks showed as much. Apparently I was rather pale and my mother took me to our doctor, who gave me a cursory examination.

' "It's his age, Madame Bureau. This boy is a bit anaemic."

'I think I felt I wasn't entirely in the real world. I wanted to get away. Not to get away from possible punishment, but get away from my parents, the town, go very far away, anywhere at all . . .'

'Are you thirsty?' Maigret asked; he was thirsty himself.

He poured two cognacs with water and held one out to his visitor, who drank greedily, emptying his glass in a breath.

'When did you become aware of what was happening to you?'

'You believe me, don't you?'

'I believe you.'

'I've always been convinced that no one would believe me . . . It happened bit by bit . . . As time passed, I felt more different from everyone else . . . Stroking my knife in my pocket, I said to myself:

' "I've killed somebody. No one knows."

'I almost wanted to tell them, to tell my fellow pupils, my teachers, my parents, the way you boast of an exploit . . . Then, one day, I caught myself following a girl along the canal. She was the daughter of some bargees, going back to her boat. It was winter, and night had already fallen . . .

'I said to myself that I would only have to take a few quick steps and take my knife out of my pocket . . .

'All of a sudden I started shaking. I turned around without thinking and ran back to the first houses in the town, as if I would feel safer there.'

'Has that happened to you often since then?'

'Since I was a child?'

'At any time.'

'About twenty times . . . In most cases I didn't have a particular victim in mind. I would be outside, and suddenly I would think:

' "I'll kill him."

'I found myself murmuring those words under my breath. They weren't directed at anyone in particular. It was just anyone.

' "I'll kill him."

'I remembered later that when I was a child, when my father smacked me and sent me to my room to punish me I would mutter the same thing:

' "I'll kill him."

'I don't suppose I could have another glass?'

Maigret poured him one, and poured one for himself at the same time.

'What age were you when you left Saint-Amand?'

'Seventeen. I knew I wouldn't pass my school leaving exam. My father didn't understand and watched me uneasily. He wanted to make me join the printworks. One night I left without a word, taking a suitcase and my modest savings.'

'And your knife!'

'Yes. A hundred times I tried to get rid of it but couldn't bring myself to do it. I don't know why. You see . . .'

He tried to find the right words. He clearly wanted to be as truthful and precise as possible, and it was difficult for him.

'In Paris, at first, I was hungry, and I ended up, like many others, unloading vegetables at Les Halles. I read the classifieds and sometimes hurried to wherever there was a job to be had. That's how I ended up working for the insurance company.'

'Did you have any steady relationships?'

'No. Every now and again I would settle for picking up a woman in the street. One of them tried to take a banknote from my wallet, and I nearly took out my knife . . . My forehead was sweating . . . I tottered away . . .

'I realized that I couldn't get married . . .'

'Did you try?'

'Have you lived alone in Paris, without parents, without friends, and come back to your lodgings all alone in the evening?'

'Yes.'

'Then you must understand. I didn't want friends either, because I couldn't be honest with them without risking prison for the rest of my days.

'I went to the Sainte-Geneviève library. I devoured psychiatric treatises, always hoping to discover an explanation. I probably lacked knowledge of the basics. When I thought that my case corresponded to a particular mental illness, I realized that I didn't have this symptom or that.

'I became more and more anxious.

' *"I'll kill him."*

'In the end I looked out for those words on my lips, and then I would run home, shut myself away and throw myself on my bed . . . Apparently I groaned . . .

'One evening, a neighbour, a middle-aged man, came and knocked at my door. I automatically took my knife out of my pocket.

' "What is it?" I asked through the door.

' "Is everything all right? Are you ill? I thought I heard groaning. I'm sorry . . ."

'He went away.'

8.

Madame Maigret appeared in the doorway and gave him a sign which he didn't understand, so far removed was it from this atmosphere, then she murmured:

'Would you come here for a moment?'

In the kitchen, she whispered:

'Dinner's ready. It's after eight. What shall we do?'

'What do you mean?'

'We need to eat.'

'It isn't over.'

'Perhaps he could eat with us?'

He looked at her, dumbfounded. For a moment her suggestion even struck him as quite natural.

'No. We don't need a laid table, a family dinner. It would make him horribly uncomfortable. Do you have any cold meat or cheese?'

'Yes.'

'In that case make some sandwiches and serve them with a bottle of white wine.'

'How is he?'

'Calmer and more lucid than I feared. I'm beginning to understand why he didn't get in touch all day. He needed to take a step back.'

'From what?'

'From himself. Did you hear?'

'At fourteen and a half he killed a boy . . .'

When Maigret came back into the living room, Robert Bureau, embarrassed, murmured:

'I'm keeping you from your dinner, aren't I?'

'If we were at Quai des Orfèvres I'd have sandwiches and beer sent up. There's no reason not to do the same thing here. My wife is making us sandwiches and she will serve them with a bottle of white wine.'

'If I'd known . . .'

'If you'd known what?'

'That someone might understand me. You're probably an exception. The examining magistrate won't have the same attitude, and neither will the jury. I've spent my life being afraid, afraid of striking again, without intending to . . .

'I watched myself all the time, in a sense, wondering if I wasn't about to have an attack. At the slightest headache, for example . . .

'I've seen I don't know how many doctors . . . I didn't admit the truth to them, of course, but I complained of violent headaches accompanied by a cold sweat. Most of them didn't take it seriously and prescribed aspirin.

'A neurologist in Boulevard Saint-Germain gave me an electro-encephalogram. According to him there's nothing wrong with my brain.'

'Was that recently?'

'Two years ago. I almost wanted to whisper to him that I wasn't normal, that I'm sick. Since he couldn't work it out by himself.

'Sometimes when I passed by a police station I wanted to go in and say:

' "I killed a kid when I was fourteen . . . I feel I risk killing again . . . It needs to be cured . . . Lock me up . . . Have me looked after . . ." '

'Why didn't you?'

'Because I read the crime pages. At almost every trial, psychiatrists give statements, and often people make fun of them. When they talk about diminished responsibility or mental illness, the jury doesn't take it into account. At best it reduces the sentence to fifteen or twenty years.

'I tried to muddle through on my own, to feel the attacks coming, to run and lock myself away at home . . . That worked for a long time . . .'

Madame Maigret brought them a tray of sandwiches, a bottle of Pouilly Fuissé and two glasses.

'Bon appétit.'

She withdrew discreetly to go and eat alone in the kitchen.

'Help yourself.'

The wine was cold and dry.

'I don't know if I'm hungry. There are days when I barely touch food, others, on the contrary, when I feel terrible hunger. That may be a sign as well. I look for signs everywhere. I analyse all my responses. I attach importance to my slightest thoughts.

'Try to put yourself in my place. At any moment I could . . .'

He bit into his sandwich and was the first to be surprised to find himself eating normally.

'And to think I was afraid of being wrong about you. I had read in the papers that you were humane and that sometimes brought you into conflict with the public prosecutor's office. On the other hand, they also talked about how you make people talk during interrogations. You treat the accused gently and cordially to win his trust and he doesn't realize that you're gradually drawing the truth out of him.'

Maigret couldn't help smiling.

'Not all cases are the same.'

'When I called you, I weighed each of your words, each of your silences . . .'

'You finally came forward.'

'I no longer had any choice. I felt that everything was collapsing . . . Wait! Let me confess something to you. Yesterday, at one point, on the Grands Boulevards, the idea came to me of attacking some random person in the midst of the crowd, to strike out around me, wildly, in the hope of getting myself shot down . . .

'Can I pour myself some more?'

He added, with slightly sad resignation:

'I won't be able to drink anything like this for the rest of my days . . .'

For a moment, Maigret tried to imagine what Poiret's face would have been like if he had been able to witness this exchange.

Bureau went on:

'There were three days of torrential rain . . . People often talk about the moon in relation to people like me. I have observed myself. I haven't noticed my impulses being more frequent or stronger when the moon is full.

'Instead what counts is a certain intensity. In July, when it's very hot, for example. In winter, when big snowflakes fall . . .

'It's as if nature is going through a crisis and . . .

'Do you understand?

'That incessant rain, the squalls, the noise of the wind shaking the shutters of my bedroom, it all put my nerves on edge.

'In the evening I left my lodgings and started walking through the storm. After a few minutes I was drenched, and I deliberately lifted my head to receive the sheets of water fully in my face.

'I didn't hear the signal or, if I did, I didn't obey . . . I should have gone home rather than carrying on . . . I didn't look where I was going . . . I walked and walked . . . Eventually my hand gripped the knife in my pocket . . .

'I saw the lights of a little bar in quite a dark street . . . I heard footsteps in the distance but they didn't worry me . . .

'A young man in a light-coloured jacket came out, with his long hair plastered to the back of his neck, and something clicked . . .

'I didn't know him. I'd never seen him before. I couldn't see his face . . . I stabbed him several times . . . Then, as I left the scene, I realized that the relief hadn't come, and I retraced my steps to stab him again and lift his head.

'That's why they talked about a frenzied attacker. They also talked about a madman.'

He fell silent and looked around him, as if surprised by the setting in which he found himself.

'I'm definitely mad, aren't I? There's no way I'm not sick . . . If someone could cure me . . . That's been my hope for so long . . . But you'll see, they'll just settle for sending me to jail for the rest of my days.'

Maigret didn't dare to reply.

'You're not saying anything?'

'I'd like you to receive treatment.'

'You don't really expect it to happen, do you?'

Maigret drained his glass.

'Drink up. In a little while we'll go to Quai des Orfèvres.'

'Thank you for listening to me.'

He emptied his glass in one, and Maigret topped it up.

Bureau hadn't been wrong about much. At the Court of Assizes, two psychiatrists came and declared that the accused was not insane in the legal sense of the word, but that his responsibility was largely diminished because he found it difficult to resist his impulses.

The lawyer begged the jury to send his client to a psychiatric hospital, where he could be kept under surveillance.

The jury accepted the attenuating circumstances but still sentenced Robert Bureau to fifteen years' imprisonment.

After which the judge cleared his throat and said:

'We realize that this verdict does not correspond completely to reality. At present, alas, we have no establishments where a man like Bureau could be treated effectively while remaining under strict surveillance.'

In the dock, Bureau looked around for Maigret and gave him a resigned smile. He seemed to say:

'I predicted this, didn't I?'

When Maigret left, his shoulders were a little heavier than before.

OTHER TITLES IN THE SERIES

MAIGRET'S PICKPOCKET
GEORGES SIMENON

'*Maigret would have found it difficult to formulate an opinion of him. Intelligent, yes, certainly, and highly so, as far as one could tell from what lay beneath some of his utterances. Yet alongside that, there was a naïve, rather childish side to him.*'

Maigret is savouring a beautiful spring morning in Paris when an aspiring film-maker draws his attention to a much less inspiring scene, one where ever changing loyalties can have tragic consequences.

Translated by Sian Reynolds

INSPECTOR MAIGRET

OTHER TITLES IN THE SERIES

MAIGRET HESITATES
GEORGES SIMENON

'Maigret looked at him in some confusion, wondering if he was dealing with a skilful actor or, on the contrary, with a sickly little man who found consolation in a subtle sense of humour.'

A series of anonymous letters lead Maigret into the wealthy household of an eminent lawyer and a curious game of cat and mouse with Paris high society.

Translated by Howard Curtis

www.penguin.com

OTHER TITLES IN THE SERIES

MAIGRET IN VICHY
GEORGES SIMENON

'What else did they have to do with their days? They ambled around casually. From time to time, they paused, not because they were out of breath, but to admire a tree, a house, the play of light and shadow, or a face.'

While taking a much-needed rest cure in Vichy with his wife, Maigret feels compelled to help with a local investigation, unravelling the secrets of the spa town's elegant inhabitants.

Translated by Ros Schwartz

OTHER TITLES IN THE SERIES